The Spying Heart

BOOKS BY KATHERINE PATERSON

Angels & Other Strangers

Bridge to Terabithia

Come Sing, Jimmy Jo

Consider the Lilies
(with John Paterson)

The Crane Wife
(translator)

Gates of Excellence

The Great Gilly Hopkins

Jacob Have I Loved

The Master Puppeteer

Of Nightingales That Weep

Park's Quest

Rebels of the Heavenly Kingdom

The Sign of the Chrysanthemum

The Spying Heart

The Tongue-cut Sparrow
(translator)

Katherine Paterson

The Spying Heart

MORE THOUGHTS
ON READING AND WRITING
BOOKS FOR CHILDREN

LODESTAR BOOKS   E. P. DUTTON   NEW YORK

Library of Congress Cataloging-in-Publication Data
Paterson, Katherine.
  The spying heart: more thoughts on reading and writing books
for children/by Katherine Paterson.
    p.   cm.
  Summary: In speeches, essays, and book reviews, the novelist
Katherine Paterson discusses why she writes children's books, where
her ideas come from, how she develops her characters and realistic
plots, and her experiences growing up in China.
  ISBN 0-525-67267-2, hardcover edition
  ISBN 0-525-67269-9, paper edition
  1. Paterson, Katherine—Authorship.   2. Children's literature—
Authorship.   3. Children—Books and reading.   [1. Paterson, Katherine.
2. Authors. American.   3. Authorship.   4. Books and reading.]   I. Title.
PS3566.A779Z475   1988   88-17686
813'.54—dc19   CIP
                                                                  AC
Published in the United States by Lodestar Books,
an affiliate of Dutton Children's Books,
a division of Penguin Books USA Inc.

Published simultaneously in Canada
by Fitzhenry & Whiteside Limited, Toronto

Editor: Virginia Buckley   Designer: Riki Levinson

Printed in the U.S.A.
10 9 8 7 6 5 4 3 2

for
Balmer Kelly
and
Inez Morton Wager

CONTENTS

The Spying Heart

The Story of My Lives

The title I had chosen for my remarks was "The Story of My Lives." I took a look at the title and decided that perhaps I should propose an alternative that sounds less like a description of a personality disorder. So I do have an alternate title. I got this one from a note card that lives in my desk drawer. The card has a three-panel illustration. At the top lies a zonked-out whale with Xs where his eyes should be. Below is the same whale with his eyes popped in amazement as a voice coming from its mouth declares: "Incredible as it seems . . ." In panel three the sentence is completed by a person who is climbing out of the whale's mouth: ". . . my life is based on a true story."[1]

Well, incredible as it seems, my life is based on a true story. Sometimes it is incredible even to me. In February I spent two weeks in England. I could spend all my allotted time telling you about that trip—tea with Rosemary Sutcliff, twice; long, relaxed visits with Jan Mark, Clive King, John Rowe Townsend, Jill Paton Walsh; and lunch with Philippa Pearce right across the street from Tom's Midnight Garden, which you'll be happy to know still exists. I guess the incredibility of my life truly hit me the day I sat sipping a glass of Madeira, which in itself seemed something of an exotic experience.

My dear friends Jean Little, Jill Paton Walsh, and John Rowe Townsend were there. And so was the ninety-five-year-old Lucy Boston, because the room in which we were sipping the Madeira was the dining room of the 850-year-old house most of us recognize by the name Green Knowe.

Well, as one of my friends said recently, "Katherine has given up name-dropping and moved on to place-dropping." Indeed, but can't you sympathize? There I was with those people in that setting—me! I was like the man in *The New Yorker* cartoon who sits at the telephone before his huge office window overlooking the Manhattan skyline, and he is saying, "And, Mama, would you call Miss Simpson, my third-grade teacher, and tell *her* I made it to the top?"[2]

I think it is my fourth-grade teacher I wish I could contact. The one who counted my spelling words wrong whenever I used the Palmer method of penmanship that had been forced on me in my previous school instead of the Locker method she adhered to.

The fourth grade was a time of almost unmitigated terror and humiliation for me. I recognize now that some of my best writing had its seeds in that awful year. But I can't remember once saying to myself at nine, "Buck up, old girl, someday you're going to make a mint out of this misery."

But there are two people whom I remember with great fondness from that horrible year. One was the librarian of Calvin H. Wiley School who, I'm afraid, died long before I could let her know what she meant to me. And there was Eugene Hammett, the other weird kid in the fourth grade.

There was a difference between me and Eugene. I was weird by no choice of my own. My parents had been missionaries in China, and we'd just fled from the war there. I spoke English as my friends in Shanghai had, with something of a British accent. I could hardly afford to buy lunch, much less clothes, so from time to time my classmates would recognize on my back something they had earlier donated to charity. On December 7, the Japanese attacked Pearl Harbor, and because it was known that I had come from that part of the world, there were dark hints that I might be one of *them.*

Eugene, on the other hand, was weird by choice—or mostly by choice: I guess he didn't choose his looks. He was a perfectly round little boy who wore full-moon steel-rimmed glasses long before John Lennon made them acceptable, and sported a half-inch blond brush cut. My only ambition in the fourth grade was to become somehow less weird. Eugene's declared ambition was to become a ballet dancer. In North Carolina in 1941, little boys—even well-built or skinny little boys—did not want to be ballet dancers when they grew up.

Now, sometimes outcasts despise even each other, but Eugene and I did not. We were friends for the rest of fourth grade and all of fifth, sixth, and seventh grades. During my public school career, Calvin H. Wiley was the only school I went to for two years running, and by the time Eugene and I were in the seventh grade, I had fulfilled my modest ambition. I was no longer regarded as particularly weird. Eugene, having more integrity, continued to march, or should I say dance, to a different drummer.

I moved the summer after seventh grade. I grew up at last and had a full, rich life in which people loved me and didn't call me names, at least not to my face. But from time to time over the years I would think of Eugene and worry about him. Whatever could have happened to my chubby little friend whose burning desire in life was to become a ballet dancer?

Decades pass. There are a lot of scene changes. We are living in Norfolk, Virginia, and our son David has become, at seventeen, a serious actor. But in order to get the parts he wants, he realizes he needs to take dancing lessons. There is, however, a problem. Even in 1983, boys in Norfolk, Virginia, do not generally aspire to become ballet dancers. He asks me to find out about lessons he can take without the rest of the soccer team knowing about it.

My friend Kathryn Morton's daughter takes ballet, so I say to Kathryn, "David needs to take ballet lessons, but he's not eager for all his buddies to know about it. Do you have any recommendations?"

"Well," says Kathryn, "if he's really serious, Gene Hammett at Tidewater Ballet is really the best teacher anywhere around. You may think he's strange but—"

"W-w-w-wait a minute," I say. "Gene who?"

"Hammett," she says. "He sends dancers to the Joffrey and New York City Ballet and Alvin Ailey every year. He's especially good with young black dancers. Terribly hard on any kid that he thinks has talent, but he'd give his life for them."

"Gene who?" I say again.

"Hammett," she says. "You may have seen him around town. He's huge and wears great flowing caftans. He does look a bit weird, but he's a wonderful teacher."

"You don't happen to know where he came from?"

"Well, he came here from New York."

"New York? He wasn't a dancer?"

"Oh, yes. He was quite good in his time. You wouldn't know it by looking at him now, but he was a fine dancer twenty, thirty years ago."

"You wouldn't happen to know where he grew up?"

"Oh, I don't know," she says. "North Carolina somewhere, I think."

"Next time you see him, would you ask him if he remembers anyone named Katherine Womeldorf from Calvin H. Wiley School?"

Some days later the phone rings. "Katherine?" an unfamiliar male voice begins. "This is Gene Hammett."

"Eugene! Do you remember me?"

"I even remember a joke you told me in the fourth grade. I asked you why if you were born in China you weren't Chinese. And you said; 'If a cat's born in a garage, does it make it an automobile?' "

"Yep," I say, recognizing one of our family defensive lines. "And what about you? You danced in New York and now you're a famous teacher of ballet. It's hard to imagine. You were a little round boy when I knew you."

He laughs. "Well," he says, "now I'm a big round man."

I have since seen Eugene, and he *is* a big round man. But I have also seen pictures of him leaping like Baryshnikov from the boards of a New York stage, thin and muscled and bearing no resemblance whatsoever to the chubby, bespectacled boy in my mind's eye. And even if I missed knowing him when he was slim and gorgeous and at the height of his career, I wouldn't give anything for knowing that it happened as he had determined it would back there when we were both weird little nine-year-olds at Calvin H. Wiley School.

Yes, incredible as it seems, my life is based on a true story, but rarely does it have such a satisfying plot line. That's the trouble with life. It tends to be deficient when it comes to offering up adequate plots. I'm sure that's why I resist writing an autobiography. As hard as it is for me to come up with a decent plot, I'm fascinated by a good one, and life, even my incredible one, offers so few well-rounded stories like the one about Gene Hammett. Thus, in a real sense, I am constantly writing autobiography, but I have to turn it into fiction in order to give it credibility. "She lived to tell the tale," we say. Because what we applaud is not simply survival but the ability to step back, or beyond survival, to organizing the experience—to imaging—to telling the tale.

If you are observant, you will have noticed that in both my proposed title and my alternate, the word *story* is singular. The singular was a deliberate choice, based on literary research and not on a deficiency of grammar. It comes from having read *The Hero with a Thousand Faces*.

In this book Joseph Campbell reduces the multitude of the world's myths, legends, and folk tales to a single story—that of the hero who ventures forth from the ordinary world into a realm of wonders. There he is met by a supernatural guide who aids him as he confronts and defeats fabulous forces and returns a victor, able to bestow boons on his fellows. I think somewhere in the backs of our minds, we writers agree. We may write many books, but there is a common thread. It may not fit Campbell's formula exactly, but we cannot deny the kinship.

When I was in England, my British editor asked me what I was working on. She did it very delicately, which made me think that as she asked she was hoping against hope that I was not doing another of those dadgum historical novels that she, being a loyal sort of editor, would probably go ahead and print and then have trouble selling. And I heard myself answering, "Oh, you know, Chris, it's the same old thing I always do."

Which, come to think of it, is not a very clever way to advertise your nearly finished book to a publisher you hope will love it. But actually, when pressed, it is hard to put into a sentence or two exactly what that "same old thing" is. So I asked myself, as someone who goes to great pains to set her stories in different countries at different periods of history, and who resists all pressures to write a sequel, What on earth did I mean by "the same old thing"?

Well, if you promise not to write a dissertation on it, I'll let you in on what, as of this moment, I think it might mean. I went to church twice on Ash Wednesday and as a reward for my unusual diligence, I was given what may be a key to the story of my fictional lives.

We were discussing the feast liturgy of ancient Israel and read what has long been a favorite line of mine from the Book of Deuteronomy. I guess I should put the line in context.

At the feast of the first fruits, the worshiper is to take a basket of the first of all his fruits and give it to the priest. The priest sets down the basket at the altar, and then the worshiper is to say:

A wandering Aramean was my father; and he went down into Egypt and sojourned there, few in number; and there he became a nation, great, mighty, and populous. And the Egyptians treated us harshly, and afflicted us, and laid upon us hard bondage. Then we cried to the Lord the God of our fathers, and the Lord heard our voice, and saw our affliction, our toil, and our oppression; and the Lord brought us out of Egypt with a mighty hand and an outstretched arm, with great terror, with signs and wonders; and he brought us into this place and gave us this land, a land flowing with milk and honey. And behold, now I bring the first of the fruit of the ground, which thou, O Lord, hast given me.[3]

As I study this passage, it seems to echo Joseph Campbell's archetypal story—but the language, the feel of the words themselves does something to my insides. "A wandering Aramean was my father." Do you realize how much effort is expended by characters in my books looking for the wandering father and, occasionally, the mother? And if the child knows just where his or her parents are, geographically speaking, it is the child who is wandering, either physically or spiritually. And the wandering, whether it be the parent's or the child's, takes the child of my story into some sort of bondage.

James Johnson fits very nicely into this scheme I'm proposing. He is not only a wanderer—witness the song he loves, "I'm Just a Poor Wayfaring Stranger"—but both of his fathers and his mother are wayfarers. He travels down to Tidewater and into the bondage of the General Douglas MacArthur Elementary School. There, with the aid of a supernatural helper, he overcomes the foes within and without and wins the victory that enables him to give his gift to his fellows.

Oh, you're wondering about that supernatural helper? I didn't know he had one either, but it occurred to me to look up the meaning of the name *Eleazer*—long after I had given James's friend that name. Sometimes we write more truly than we know. The name *Eleazer* means "God has helped."

If the helpers of the heroes of my other stories have less blatantly supernatural names, everyone has at least one helper. Muna has the swordsmith, Takiko has the Empress, Jiro has Kinshi, Gilly has Trotter, Louise has the Captain, Wang Lee has Mei Lin and Chu—and Shen, whom he betrays. Jesse has Leslie, who is the quintessential helper, but who—like all the helpers in my books—is in fact mortal, which means that Jesse's father and Mrs. Myers must come to his aid before the battle is done.

But as a novelist, it is the mortal that matters to me. My stories, like all stories, may be ultimately descended from the story of the princely hero with a thousand faces, but their father is a wandering Aramean.

That means that the battles my fictional lives must confront are not against fabulous forces. There's not, alas, a dragon in the entire body of my work. It's not that I wouldn't like to write about dragons. It's that I don't know how.

Maybe someday I'll figure out how, but at the moment fantasy is to my writing what downhill skiing is to my athletic life—strictly a spectator sport.

I'm always interested when people say to me, "Why don't you write fantasy?" Or, "Why don't you write mystery stories?" Or, "What we need for you to write are plays that children can perform in school." As though the only reason I have never done what they're suggesting is that no one had been wise enough to present the idea to me before, and I myself had not been clever enough to think of it. The reason, in case you're interested, that I don't do a lot of things is not that I haven't considered them, but that the gift I have been given is a limited one.

It is, however, a gift that I am very grateful for and that I seek to employ as responsibly as I am able. I don't get to write about the godlike heroes. I get to write about the wandering Arameans. I get to write about real people who must confront the messy battles of the world as we know it.

Last year in Minnesota a group of parents asked their district board of education to ban *The Great Gilly Hopkins* on the basis of what they saw as its anti-Christian bias, its profanity, and its "pervasive vulgarity."

"It isn't a question of censorship or no censorship but a question of where we're going to draw the line," said one of the protesters. "God," he continued, "does have a standard, and we all have to answer to him."

Now, when I wrote *Gilly Hopkins,* it occurred to me to wonder if my secular publishing house would reject it because it seemed to me so blatant a rewriting of the parable of the Prodigal Son.

In Maine more recently, a teacher was called before a

school board to defend her use of *Bridge to Terabithia* in her fifth-grade classroom. The book was being attacked not only for its profanity but for the hint of sexual feelings that the boy has for his teacher and for the references to magic and praying to spirits.

I want you to know that I do not take these complaints lightly. I do not put words or scenes into books just to make life harder for teachers and librarians. I am trying to tell a true story about real people. The fact that I call myself a Christian and see my work as a calling from God does not make people who wish to ban my books very happy. Nor could I succeed in explaining to them my belief that if I tried to write books according to their guidelines, I would be untrue to the gift that God has given me.

Flannery O'Connor, who was a devout Catholic as well as a fine writer, expresses this conviction better than I can. She says, "Fiction is about everything human and we are made out of dust, and if you scorn getting yourself dusty, then you shouldn't write fiction. It isn't grand enough for you."[4]

A wandering Aramean was my father. In Deuteronomy the wanderer is not named, but we can tell from the context that he is Jacob. Not father Abraham or noble, gentle Isaac, but Jacob the trickster, the cheat, the cowardly runaway. Now, I have a love-hate relationship with Jacob. Didn't I write a whole book from Esau's point of view? I always thought Esau had a dirty deal. He was the victim of his brother Jacob's trickery and the cheated witness to his good fortune.

When I named my book *Jacob Have I Loved,* I was sure that my publisher would make me change the title. Even today perfectly sensible people will ask me why I called the book

Jacob Have I Loved when there isn't a character named Jacob in the entire book. One thing you learn pretty quickly in this business is how little people know about the Bible. I can't begin to count the number of times in 1980 that I was asked the question, "What is the title of your new book?" And when I replied, *"Jacob Have I Loved,"* exactly one person responded, "But Esau have I hated."[5]

Perhaps the fault was my own. Maybe I chose to tell the wrong story. From reading both Joseph Campbell and the Bible, it is obvious that Jacob is the hero whose story must be told. Esau is more an obstacle to be overcome than a character in his own right.

It was certainly not my original intention that anybody identify Sara Louise Bradshaw with Jacob. She was quite obviously intended to be Esau, the cheated elder twin. And yet, deep inside ourselves exists the image of the twins—two parts of one whole. The light and the dark. Jacob looks into a darkened mirror and sees Esau. Sara Louise looks into a bright mirror and sees Caroline. In order to be whole, Jacob must make peace with Esau, Sara Louise must make peace with Caroline. In life both the light and dark exist in each of us; each of us is our own twin. So finally Sara Louise, in order to be a whole person, must come to love Caroline, so that she can love both the Jacob and the Esau within herself.

Which brings us to the greatly lamented final chapters of *Jacob Have I Loved.* How many critics have fussed and fumed and cried and demanded a bit too late that they be vastly expanded or simply lopped off. In the book's defense I should like to state that as of this date no young reader has ever complained to me about those chapters. This unhappiness with the ending is distinctly a postadolescent phenomenon. The fact that I refuse to call this criticism of the ending adult or mature may suggest where my bias in this matter lies.

But now that I have become enlightened and know what my books are all about, I have decided to tackle the problem of the ending one more time.

Looking at it freshly I see that Louise, the Esau, is indeed the wandering Aramean. The Arameans were nobodies as far as the real world of Egypt and Assyria and Babylon, and later Greece and Rome, were concerned. They conquered no empires, built no pyramids. For centuries they served as the whipping boy of civilization—the "no people," as Peter says. But Louise takes it a step further. Not only does she believe she is nobody, she thinks it's all God's fault. He didn't choose her. He chose her sister instead. So she will choose deliberately not to choose God. She is wandering not as Israel wandered—toward the promised land—but away from it. And where is God while all this is going on?

Oh, but, as I have often claimed, the author has no right to tell a reader how to read her book. It is the privilege of the reader to discover what a book means for his or her particular life. The book either speaks for itself to the reader, or it fails to speak.

But, just in case, just in case it spoke and somebody out there wasn't listening, will you remember that the hero's supernatural helper may take many forms—the fairy god-mother, the crone, the dwarf, perhaps even a baby. Will you consider that if Louise had not delivered Essie's twins she might never have told her story? She might not even have known her story.

Hours later, walking home, my boots crunching on the snow, I bent my head backward to drink in the crystal stars. And clearly, as though the voice came from just behind me, I heard a melody so sweet and pure that I had to hold myself to keep from shattering:

I wonder as I wander out under the sky . . .[6]

The hero must leave home, confront fabulous dangers, and return the victor to grant boons to his fellows. Or a wandering nobody must go out from bondage through the wilderness and by the grace of God become truly someone who can give back something of what she has been given.

That—incredible as it may seem—is the story of my lives.

Growing Up Civilized

MISS MANNERS' GUIDE
TO REARING PERFECT CHILDREN
by Judith Martin

"On the subject of manners for children, many adults believe that the opposite of 'polite' is 'creative.' Poor little mannerly children, they think—how suppressed and inhibited they must be. Actually, the opposite of 'polite' is 'rude.' If you think rude children are better off emotionally than well-behaved ones, you are in luck, because there are so many of them around. . . ." With these words, the inimitable Miss Manners throws down her impeccably white glove in the cause of civilizing the world in one generation.

No one who is even slightly acquainted with Miss Manners needs to be told how thoroughly, how intelligently, and how hilariously she has conducted her affair of honor. For example, here is Miss Manners tackling the touchy subject of punishment: "It would be nice to say that the proper parent need not be concerned with proper forms of punishment, because if he or she has properly practiced proper child-rearing, there will be no crimes to punish. Even Miss Manners doesn't dream she could get away with that. Besides, her respect for civilization itself, which it is the goal of child-rearing to instill, is so great that she does not believe it can be absorbed without a struggle. Show her a child who has never rebelled against becoming civilized, and she will show you a child who isn't smart enough to realize what those people are trying to do to him."

As you see, Miss Manners can manage the tricky feat of being an idealist and a realist at the same time. This is best illustrated by her willingness to advise families as they are and not as she might wish they were. In the section titled "Unpaired Parents," there are discussions of such practical concerns as the mannerly way to conduct the custody weekend and the etiquette required from and toward the parent's live-in companion. The chapter on weddings also provides help for multiple-parented brides and grooms.

There is, of course, the obligatory section on manners while eating, in which are reviewed not only topics Emily Post might have covered, but such helpful extras as how to lick an ice cream cone and what to do about a tablemate who swipes your french fries.

As an adoptive parent who has had her share of rude questions over the past twenty years, I was particularly gratified with Miss Manners' help for those of us who would like to maintain family grace while under boorish attack. To the mother of a handicapped son who must constantly deal with persons whose "curiosity outweighs their intelligence," Miss Manners wisely replies:

"GENTLE READER: Miss Manners is gratified that you are willing to deal with the reality of the situation, which is that people always will be asking those rude questions, and that there is no percentage in your son's learning to return the rudeness. You do not even mention the rudeness of being asked questions about your son in front of him, as if he were an object, which Miss Manners finds appalling, too.

"Only when the temporarily able-bodied come to accept disabilities as a common human condition will we have a truly civilized society. In the meantime, you must continue, politely and firmly, to refuse to satisfy unseemly curiosity about his person. Miss Manners suggests you meet all questions with the cheerful statement, 'Oh, the braces are utilitarian. I assure you, he doesn't just wear them for decorative purposes.' "

There is a danger in immersing oneself in Miss Manners' style and substance. The humble reviewer may become doused with delusions of grandeur. . . .

DEAR MS. REVIEWER: Just two years ago, at great personal sacrifice, I went out and bought *Miss Manners' Guide to Excruciatingly Correct Behavior,* and I am a constant reader of her syndicated column. Should I pawn the family ruby to buy her new book, or is it mostly reruns of the above?

GENTLE BUYER: By all means, pawn the family ruby. In the first place, Miss Manners' late grandmother considered colored stones tacky, and in the second, like the virtuous woman in the Book of Proverbs, Miss Manners' price is "far above rubies." Yes, there is some overlapping, but Miss Manners maintains that the two chief tools of child-rearing are example and nagging. You wouldn't want her to set a bad example by never repeating herself, now would you? Besides, the illustrations alone make this book worth the family jewel. [Note to the publisher: Please do not prosecute anyone who photocopies Gloria Kamen's illustrations. Every parent striving for adequacy will find it necessary to hang a copy of page 4, "Essential Parental Facial Expressions" (including "just wait till the company leaves"), beside the bathroom mirror. And the absolutely delectable double spread "Wardrobes for Proper Children," pages 118–119, being done as it is in paper-doll style, is guaranteed to tempt beyond endurance some not yet perfect child into taking her scissors to the page.]

DEAR MS. REVIEWER: I don't have any children. What's more, I don't even like children. Do I need this book?

GENTLE BUYER: Yes. Or perhaps you haven't noticed the number of persons under five feet tall who regard you with quiet, polite humor and a fixed smile.

DEAR MS. REVIEWER: I hate to seem picky, but don't you think the subtitle of Miss Manners' new book: "A Primer for Everyone Worried about the Future of Civilization" just the teeniest bit pretentious?

GENTLE BUYER: Absolutely not. If only the leaders of the world would listen to Miss Manners. "Ideological differences are no excuse for rudeness," she says, and I'm sure, knowing her as I do, that she considers name-calling, threats, and assorted rattling of missiles exceedingly rude. Miss Manners emphasizes that manners have to do, not with how you feel, which is your own business, but with how you behave, which is everyone's concern. If we could all learn how to behave politely, the future of civilization, not to mention the planet, would be considerably brighter.

from the *Washington Post Book World*
October 21, 1984

Ideas

The writer of an article about Dr. Seuss reported that at the end of an interview Theodore Geiss congratulated him for not asking the one question that people invariably ask. When the writer asked him what that one question might be, Dr. Seuss replied, "Where do you get your ideas?" "Well, all right," said the reporter. "Where *do* you get your ideas?" "I'm glad you asked that," Dr. Seuss said and pulled out a printed card. On the card was spelled out the secret that the world pants for. It seems that on the stroke of midnight at the full moon of the summer solstice, Dr. Seuss makes an annual pilgrimage into the desert, where an ancient Native American hermit and wise man has his abode. That old Indian, Dr. Seuss declared, is the source of all his ideas. But where the old Indian gets *his* ideas, he has no notion.

Where do you get your ideas? I suppose the people who ask this question are expecting a rational, one-sentence reply. What they get from me is a rather stupid stare. Unlike the good doctor, I have no earthly notion of how to answer this question. My impulse is to retort rudely, "Where do you get *your* ideas?" I've never met anyone devoid of ideas. Of course, a lot of ideas are bad or dumb. Indeed, a lot of *my* ideas are bad or dumb, but I try not to publish those. What is the questioner asking for? Does he want geography, history, philosophy? Is he asking for a chart of my inner space with a star at the spot where ideas come from?

It occurred to me in the middle of all these ravings that I might be doing what the mother of the old story did when her Johnny asked where he came from. She took a deep breath and spent fifteen minutes initiating her six-year-old into the mysteries of human birth. At the end of which Johnny said, "Well, I was just wondering. Billy said he came from Philadelphia."

There are, after all, some answers to the question, Where do you get your ideas? that are not lost in the nether regions of my subconscious. I can remember, for example, a lot of things that led to the writing of *The Great Gilly Hopkins.* It began initially because I wanted to write a funny story. No, there was something even before that. It occurred in the spring of 1975 while I was hard at work on *Bridge to Terabithia.* Events on the other side of the world were invading my peaceful living room every night. Vietnam fell and then Cambodia. My children were watching the films of the homeless children and saying, "Can't we help? Don't we have room for some more children?" And I was saying, "I can't take care of more than four children. We can't possibly afford another child." But finally I agreed with the family's feeling that if we couldn't adopt any more, we could certainly provide temporary foster care. Since we had been certified as genuine okay parents by the local Lutheran Social Service when we adopted Mary, we were asked to take in two Cambodian boys for two weeks. That didn't seem so hard. We bought a bunk bed so we could turn the boys' bedroom into a dormitory, and I started cooking rice three times a day, thinking how lucky these boys were to come into the home of a woman who knew how to cook rice properly. Well, it wasn't as easy as cooking rice. The two weeks stretched into two more weeks and then two more and two more. The honeymoon period, when everyone was on his or her best behavior, was all too quickly over. I learned a lot about children, about being a foster parent, and about myself that, given the choice, I'd just as soon not have learned. I had always thought of myself as a B— or at the least a C+ mother, and here I was flunking.

I had to ask myself why. And I found the answer in my attitude. When I first met each of our four children, either in the delivery room or at the airport, I knew this child was mine—that there was no backing out for either of us. No matter what happened, for better or worse, in sickness or in health, as long as we both lived, we would belong to each other as parent and child. This sort of absolute conviction does something to a relationship, and both you and the child know it. When problems arise, you know there's no escape, so you work them out. But with foster children, there's no such conviction. I would find myself thinking, I can't really deal with that. They'll be here such a short time. Or, Thank heavens this is only temporary! And what I was doing was regarding another human being as a disposable commodity. Now, I am quite aware of the fact that there is nothing funny about this attitude. I am also aware of the thousands of foster children in this country who have to live out their lives in a world that regards them as disposable, and it took me quite a while to realize that the funny book I wanted to write was buried in this tragic idea.

It was the summer after the boys left us for their adoptive homes that I started to read *The Lord of the Rings*. My apartment mate in 1961 had been a Tolkien fan, and she had wanted me to read the books back then. But I had been too busy studying theology to take on three fat volumes of fiction, so I had put it off until, suddenly, it had become a cultic act to read Tolkien, and I have never been one to join a cult. Finally, that July, exhausted from writing *Bridge* and trying to be a foster mother, I took the books to Lake George and began to read.

I remember vividly the day I came to the end of *The Return of the King*. Sam, as you will remember, has gone to Grey Havens to see Frodo off on the mysterious ship that will carry him away forever.

"Then Frodo kissed Merry and Pippin, and last of all Sam, and went aboard; and the sails were drawn up, and the wind blew, and slowly the ship slipped away down the long grey firth; and the light of the glass of Galadriel that Frodo bore glimmered and was lost." Tolkien then relates how the three companions return home in silence, until they part and Sam at last "came back up the hill as day was ending once more. And he went on, and there was yellow light, and fire within; and the evening meal was ready and he was expected. And Rose drew him in, and set him in his chair, and put little Elanor upon his lap.

"He drew a deep breath. 'Well, I'm back,' he said."[1]

I looked up from Sam's last words, startled to find myself in a bathing suit, sitting on a towel, shivering in the sun, with people about me chatting, and children running and splashing into the water, calling out to one another. Where was I? It took me several minutes to reorient myself, until I was no longer in Middle Earth but had made the long, long journey home.

Someday, I told myself, someday, I'm going to write a book, and the central character is going to be a girl named Galadriel. Eventually, my young heroine became Galadriel Hopkins, for a reason that only surfaced this past year. Waiting in an autograph line was a distinguished-looking man with a volume of poetry protruding from his jacket pocket: *The Collected Poems of Gerard Manley Hopkins.* Instantly I knew where Gilly had gotten her last name. Gerard Manley, like his namesake Gilly, lives in the deepest places of my soul.

Anyhow, for months I carried her about with me—Galadriel Hopkins—my child without a story.

I don't know how long I would have borne this child around unfleshed, but we have at our house one inexorable deadline. It is called Christmas Eve. Somehow, years ago, I began writing a story for my husband to read at the Christmas Eve service, and before I knew it, it had become a tradition. Every year I say, How can I possibly write another story? There are only so many themes attached to Christmas, and I've already done them all—several times. But somehow, each year, I manage one more, swearing it will be the last.

The events of the spring were still in my mind and on my conscience, and the Christmas story for 1975 was about an elderly man who takes in two foster children for Christmas. The old man is full of love and generosity, but something terrible happens. The recipients of his compassion *are not grateful.* If you have read "Maggie's Gift," you know already that once I had written it, I knew exactly who Galadriel Hopkins was. She was a foster child, born to a flower child who had read all of Tolkien, but who was still too much of a child herself to care for a real live child of her own. Not a funny subject—but there you are—these were the ideas that came together for the funny book I wanted to write.

Whenever I repeat a word often enough, I realize how dimly I understand its meaning. What exactly is an idea? I try to define it, and the image that pops into mind is the comic-book balloon with the light bulb inside. You can't talk to teachers and librarians in comic-book images, so I went, magnifying glass in hand, to my *Compact Edition of the Oxford English Dictionary.* It was like telling Johnny where he came from. Even in print that you have to read with a magnifying glass, the word *idea* consumes sixteen and a half inches. The esteemed editors take us back to the Greek origins—where *idea* is the general or ideal form, the archetype, as opposed to the individual form. I kept searching for what I thought an idea was, and came upon it eventually, buried in the fourth inch. And I quote: "In weakened sense: a conception or notion of something to be done or carried out; an intention, plan of action."

It's sad to think that when I use the word *idea* I am using it in the weakened sense, but there you are. I do, however, have one advantage over some people. If a definition doesn't satisfy me in English, I can look it up in Japanese. And in Japanese, the word is *i*, which is made up of two characters —the character for *sound* and the character for *heart*—so an idea is something that makes a sound in the heart (the heart in Japanese, as in Hebrew, being the seat of intelligence as well as the seat of feeling).

Isn't that a wonderful picture? There is something lying deep within you that suddenly one day without warning sets off an alarm, rings, sounds, waking up your heart.

Now what does all this have to do with writing fiction? A great deal, it seems to me. Because I believe that in writing fiction, I must be released from the concept of idea as ideal form or archetype, I must be released from the concept of idea as notion or plan of action, and I must cling to those ideas for fiction that are truly sounds from my heart.

If you are observant, you have noted that, like any good Presbyterian preacher, I have just handed you the three-point outline of my sermon. It seems to me, you see, that a great deal of our problem with fiction, especially fiction for children, stems from the fact that we don't know what fiction is. I will proceed, therefore, to tell you, captive audience that you are, what I believe fiction to be.

A novel, first of all, deals only indirectly with ideal forms or archetypes. Myths and fairy tales deal directly with archetypes, and there is a very real place for them, especially as they help children to map the dark regions of their souls, to face and conquer their inner dragons. We cannot, we must not, deprive children of these powerful images. Without them, not only do art and literature lose their power, but the soul itself stands ravaged and windowless like a vandalized cathedral.

But a novel, while it has its roots in the ancient stories, is not the same thing. It is much more humble, perhaps the least lofty of all the arts. In fiction, you see, our medium is not the archetypal forms but human experience, which is truth at a very earthly level. If we are told in Genesis 1 that God created us male and female in God's own image, on the very next page, we are told that we were created from the dust of the earth. Now, most of us high-minded people who want to write fiction are very happy with the idea of Genesis 1, but we get most uncomfortable when we turn from the august and the abstract and find ourselves in the mud by the creek bank. It is not simply the behavior of real live people or even the language of real live children that we shy away from. It is the fact that in fiction, the writer does not dress up grand ideas in human form, she *starts* with the human being—who may very well have torn cuticles and B.O. but who, at best, is a mortal creature that tastes, smells, hears, touches, sees, and somewhere down the line begins to conceptualize and believe. A person in a novel can certainly *have* ideas, but if the idea has the person, we are not looking at truth but at propaganda.

I have been very aware of this first misunderstanding of fiction in the varied responses I've gotten to *The Great Gilly Hopkins.* I got a terrifying letter from a teacher telling me how much she liked the book because, she said, Gilly is such a wonderful role model for today's children. Well, I don't know about you, but I don't want for my children a role model who lies, steals, takes advantage of the handicapped, bullies the weak, acts out her racial bigotry in a particularly tasteless fashion, and regularly takes the name of the Lord in vain. I do not personally approve of any of these forms of behavior. I am not, in *Gilly,* trying to tell anyone how I think children *ought* to behave. I am trying to tell the story of a lost child who is angry with the world that regards her as disposable and who is fighting it with every available weapon—fair or foul.

And, when, on the other hand, I am accused of writing less than the ideal book, when I am taken to task for Gilly's cursing—never, alas, for all her other sins, just her cursing —when I am asked the painful question, "Couldn't the book have been just as effective without profanity?" I have to say, "No, I do not see how it could have been." We all know that a child who lies, steals, bullies, and acts out her racial bigotry with vicious ferocity—we all know that this child does not say "fiddlesticks" when frustrated. If Gilly is to be believed, her mouth must reflect the lost child within. Of course, if the book had faithfully reproduced the language of the Gillys some of us know all too well, the weight of obscenity would have totally unbalanced the story. Such, you see, is the power of words, and the writer must be aware of this power and walk gently.

Which brings us to the second definition of *idea* and the second point I want to make about fiction—that is, fiction as notion or plan of action. I am quite aware that I have been accused of writing didactic books that try to foist lessons and values on unsuspecting little minds (which would mean that I have violated my own guidelines by erring in the direction of the ideal rather than the true), but I have also been accused (in reviews of the very same book) of this second sin—that of being too practical and down to earth—of writing so-called problem fiction. Now, what is problem fiction and what is the problem with it?

Let me use one of my own books to illustrate. Sara Louise Bradshaw has this big problem. She is jealous of her gorgeous, talented sister. So the plan of action—the plot, if you please—of this book is to solve Sara Louise's problem. The first thing most of us ever learned about writing fiction is that conflict is at its very heart. If there is no problem, there is no story. So what am I fussing about? I am fussing about what my dictionary calls the weakened sense—the reduction of human life to a series of problems that can, with insight and a bit of doing, be solved.

The first time I was told that *Bridge to Terabithia* was "on our death list," I was a bit shaken up. There follows, you see, the feeling that if a child has a problem, a book that deals with that problem can be given to the child and the problem will be cured. As Jill Paton Walsh points out, only children's books are used this way. "One does not," she says, "rush to give *Anna Karenina* to friends who are committing adultery, or minister to distressed old age with copies of *King Lear*."[2] Still, if we look at life as a series of problems needing solving, it is hard not to offer nicely packaged, portable solutions, preferably paperback. I know. No one has given out more copies of *Ramona the Brave* to first-graders in distress than I have.

A couple of years ago, *Psychology Today* published an article on the so-called delayed stress syndrome that is appearing more and more in veterans of Vietnam. When the author, Peter Marin, began interviewing veterans and the psychologists and counselors called to deal with this stress, he found that all the traditional methods of problem solving had failed. "Our great therapeutic dream is that the past is escapable, that insight leads to joy," Marin says. But in his interviewing he found that the more insight these men obtained, the greater their anguish. They were, he said, "living in moral pain," and their therapists would not treat it, for their therapists had no cure for moral pain. "One psychologist told me he never dealt with guilt. 'We treat the vets' difficulties as problems in adjustment,' he said."[3]

I think this was the phrase that haunted me most from the article—"problems in adjustment"—as though the psychologist thought of his patient as a machine that, with the proper tinkering, could be brought once more to maximum efficiency.

Ursula Le Guin, in her Library of Congress speech entitled "The Child and the Shadow," speaks of this same shallowness in many of the so-called problem books for children. "The problem of drugs, of divorce, of race prejudice, of unmarried pregnancy, and so on—as if evil were a problem in arithmetic . . . *that* is escapism . . . posing evil as a 'problem' instead of what it is: all the pain and suffering and waste and loss and injustice we will meet all our lives long and must face and cope with over and over, and admit, and live with, in order to live human lives at all."[4]

But how are we to help children face evil? We cannot, as Le Guin goes on to say, simply give children pictures of Nazi gas chambers, or the famines of India, or the cruelties of a psychotic parent and say, " 'Well, baby, this is how it is, what are you going to make of it?' If you suggest there is a 'solution' to these monstrous facts, you are lying to a child. If you insist that there isn't, you are overwhelming him with a load he's not strong enough to handle."[5]

But what can we do? My four children have grown up

under the mushroom cloud—am I to give them teenage romance novels to soothe their fears? Recently Clyde Robert Bulla told me in a letter of visiting an elementary school. The children had made elaborate preparations for the author's visit. One of the things they presented to him was a wishing tree. When he got home and read the wishes tied to the branches, a few of them were what he expected—"I wish I had a pony"—"I wish I didn't have to go to school"—but the other wishes disturbed him deeply. The children were in grades one to four, and this is what they wished for:

"A wish for the world. That Russia doesn't drop bombs on us."

"I wish all people didn't get hurt."

"My wish is that all of the people of the world would stop all wars because it is a dumb idea. People will just kill everybody for no reason at all. They just want to have land."

"I wish that the holl world has safety."

"I wish there were no war—just peace."

The fourth grade wrote this poem:

> Dear World,
> We hope that there will be
> No children crying
> People dying
> Missiles flying
> We hope for peace
> > freedom
> > > love.

There may be some protected children somewhere who have never felt pain or grief or fear. But I haven't met any of them. The children I know are like the children who hung their wishes on Clyde Bulla's tree. Did they have to hang those wishes, like Shinto prayers, on the branches because they felt unable to speak them aloud to the adults who order their lives?

But what can we do for our children if we are neither to lie to them nor lay upon them burdens they are incapable of bearing? I think there is a hint in Peter Marin's article, in the words of one of the veterans he interviewed.

" 'I'm an artist,' he said. 'A sculptor. At least that's what I've been doing lately. Coming home from the war, I saw huge piles of shell casings. And a couple of years ago I realized that I wanted to use them to make a gigantic sculpture. Something to commemorate the dead, to let people know what the war had been like. For years I tried to get those casings. But they wouldn't let me have them. They were being recycled, they said, to make new shells. . . .'

"And suddenly he was shaking and weeping, unable to go on, crying, as vets will, at the impossibility of explaining to others what drives them.

"Later," Marin continues, "he came over to explain to me. 'I don't know how to explain it,' he said. 'I keep thinking that if I could do this one thing, if I could just get it, if I could make this one thing, then somehow it would be all right, they'd see, they'd know, and then it wouldn't happen again.' "[6]

The power of the imagination—the sound of the heart. What can we do? I think one thing we can do is to share with children works of the imagination—those sounds deepest in the human heart, often couched in symbol and metaphor. These don't give children packaged answers. They invite children to go within themselves to listen to the sounds of their own hearts.

I had wanted to write the story that became *Jacob Have I Loved* for a long time, because I knew how important the relationships between sisters or between sister and brother are, but before that idea—that notion—that problem—could become a book, at least two things had to happen. The idea had to be incarnate in a person—it had to cease being general and abstract and become individual in a child who lived in a specific place at a specific time. The book had to be researched every bit as carefully as a novel set in twelfth-century Japan. But, more important, the book had to come from the sounds within my deepest heart. I could not cheat and I could not hurry.

Someone—I think it was Goethe—once said, "The beginning and end of all literary activity is the reproduction of the world that surrounds me by means of the world that is in me. . . ."

Now, of course it is the height of arrogance to suppose that the world that is in me has any significance for you— much less for children whose experience of the world is necessarily limited. How can I ask them to see their own nuclear-threatened world through, for example, a rebellion of Chinese peasants in the middle of the nineteenth century? And yet I do, because the world that is in me is the only world I have by which to grasp the world outside, and, as I write fiction, it is the chart by which I must steer. I must never forget how limited my own experience is and how partial my vision of truth must be, but nonetheless, it is the only vision I have right now, and I must be as faithful to it as I can.

The work reveals the creator—and as our universe in its vastness, its orderliness, its exquisite detail, tells us something of the One who made it, so a work of fiction, for better or worse, will reveal the writer. There is always for me a horrible moment just before a new novel is published when I wonder if I can stand being stripped naked still another time. Someone said to me recently that she had read my books and now wanted to really get to know *me*. I didn't say it aloud. Convention keeps me quiet once in a while. But inside myself I was saying—Lady, you already know me far better than you have any right to. It is not that Wang Lee's, or Gilly Hopkins's, or Louise Bradshaw's life is a retelling of my own. Of course not. But feelings reveal more than facts. And a writer can never know about a character's feelings what is not somewhere mirrored in her own.

The poet Rilke describes what must happen. "For the sake of a single verse," he says, ". . . one must be able to think back to roads in unknown regions . . . to days of childhood that are still unexplained. . . . And still it is not yet enough to have memories. One must forget them and one must have great patience to wait until they come again. For it is not yet the memories themselves, not till they have turned to blood within us, to glance and gesture, nameless and no longer to be distinguished from ourselves—not till then can it happen that in a most rare hour the first word of a verse arises in their midst and goes forth from them."[7]

The memories must turn to blood within us before the images, ideas, the sounds of the heart can come forth.

A seventh-grader in California asked me, "What do you

want the reader to achieve by reading *Bridge to Terabithia?*" And I said to him, "Look, my job is to write the best book I know how to write. Your job is to decide what you're to achieve by reading it." A book is a cooperative venture. The writer can write a story down, but the book will never be complete until a reader of whatever age takes that book and brings to it his own story. I realize tonight, as I realize every time I speak, that I am addressing an audience that includes many of my coauthors.

So please don't ask me where I get my ideas as if I were some creature foreign to you who drinks at an alien watering trough. Don't ask me where I get my ideas as though you have no part, no responsibility, in bringing what you read to life. Frances Clarke Sayers speaks of the "shattering and gracious encounter that art affords." It is only when the deepest sound going forth from my heart meets the deepest sound coming forth from yours—it is only in this encounter that the true music begins.

An American Childhood in China

HOMESICK: MY OWN STORY
by Jean Fritz

Every now and then a book comes along that makes me want to send a valentine to its author. *Homesick* is such a book. I suppose all of us BIC's (born in China) with literary ambitions have been urged at some time or another to record our childhood experiences. Now we don't have to. Jean Fritz has done it, putting her life and ours into a story as pungent and delicious as those meat dumplings we used to buy off the peddler's cart.

Fritz, who has made her place in children's and young adult literature telling other people's stories, from Paul Revere's to Stonewall Jackson's, now turns her eye for the revealing detail and her warm humor upon herself. With a historian's devotion to accuracy, Fritz has chosen to call the account fiction, recognizing the impossibility of recalling one's past perfectly. It is a wise decision, allowing the writer to reconstruct or create (who cares?) childhood scenes complete with dialogue like the following:

" 'I know what you can give me for Christmas,' I told my mother.

" 'I've already bought your presents.' My mother was writing letters at her little black lacquer desk and she didn't look up.

" 'This wouldn't cost a thing,' I explained. 'It would be easy.'

" 'Well?' She still didn't look up.

" 'You could give me a new name. That's what I really want.'

"Now she did look up. She even put down her pen. 'And what, may I ask, is the matter with the name you have?'

". . . I put my arm around her neck because I didn't want her to feel bad about the mistake she'd made. 'Give me the name Marjorie. Just write it on a gift card and put it in a box. You see how easy it would be.'

"My mother shook her head as if she couldn't understand how I'd got into the family. 'I wouldn't name a cat Marjorie,' she said.

"Well, of course not! 'Marjorie is not a cat's name,' I yelled. And I stamped out of the room."

Almost every girl has had a similar conversation with her mother at some point between the ages of ten and sixteen. What makes Jean's request different is that it takes place in Hankow, China, in 1925. Jean Guttery was born in China and has lived there all her young life. She goes to a British school where she is pressured by a stern teacher and the class bully to sing "God Save the King," which Americans haven't been singing since George III. Jean wants to be called Marjorie because she thinks she would feel more American if her name were Marjorie. Marjories, Jean imagines, roller-skate and celebrate Halloween and live near sympathetic grandmothers. She is desperate to be a Marjorie—to feel really American. She is terribly homesick for a land she has never seen.

Meanwhile, the country of her birth is torn by riots and revolution. Arrogant foreign powers have taken over parts of its cities and erected signs: No Dogs, No Chinese. Even Jean's beloved United States has gunboats patrolling the Yangtze River. " 'In case,' " my father said. In case what? 'Just in case.' That's all he'd say."

Fritz has gotten the voice of the book exactly right. It is the voice of a bright, imaginative, funny child, straining both toward growing up and toward that rainbow country where there are no beggars or wars or Communist mobs—the place where she will no longer be an exile.

This is Jean's story, and while Fritz never wavers from the myopic view of a child in telling it, she is still able to deliver the important people in Jean's life fully rounded. There is her lovely mother who can share books and beauty, but not her own heartache with her daughter. Jean's father is a conscientious YMCA executive who has made friends at every level of Chinese society, but who takes boyish delight in breaking records and surviving Narrow Squeaks. Jean is an only child, so the household servants comprise the rest of her family. She loves her amah passionately, a love that is touchingly reciprocated. She fears the peevish cook who, against orders, carves pagodas out of butter, doing the delicate details with the two-inch-long nails on his pinkies. When the cook turns Communist, Jean suspects he is trying to poison her. Her best friend is Andrea Hull whose family is also YMCA and thus, Jean reasons, must also believe in goodness. What they stress, however, is freedom and naturalness, which leads to sleeping all together on the porch no matter what the weather, walking about unclad, and failing to divide conversations into "Adult subjects and You're-Not-Old-Enough-to-Understand subjects."

Goodness is almost as much of an obsession with Jean as America is. But, whereas she longs for America and fancies that she would make a terrific American, she decidedly does not possess a natural aptitude for goodness. Her mother never gives up urging it upon her. "Be good, sweet child, and let who will be clever," she writes in Jean's autograph book. "Dear Grandma" (Jean writes in her next letter), "I want to warn you so you won't be disappointed. I'm not always good. Sometimes I don't even try."

When Jean at last reaches America—not the land of her dreams, but the real America where classmates are ignorant and teasing, and a pompous teacher presides over that uniquely American form of torture known as the Palmer method of penmanship, it is Grandma who turns this foreign country into home. The funniest scene of the book (and there are lots of funny scenes) is the one in which Jean shares her painful first day of school with her grandmother. "And listening to my grandmother telling it, making up bits as she went along about the imaginary Mr. Palmer who was so set on exercising the underside of children's forearms, I had to laugh again. . . . My grandmother turned serious. 'You can't move your fingers at all?' she asked, as if she might not have heard right the first time.

" 'Not at all.'

"My grandmother shook her head. 'They must be preparing you for a crippled old age.' " Every child should have such a grandma.

It is important to note that *Homesick*, while it contains many vivid observations, is not a book about China. It is the personal story of an expatriate child living through a very troubled time. Jean longed to leave China because in 1925–27 it was an alien and frightening place. You cannot ask a ten-year-old to set her vision on the cultural riches of a great civilization when the sounds and smells of everyday life outside her gate are those of poverty and disease, when angry mobs threaten her family, when earnest attempts at friendship are turned back with the cry, "Foreign devil!" But as much as she longs for America and the safety and comfort it represents, young Jean realizes on leaving China that she will be forever divided. Like all the BIC's I know, she will find herself homesick on both sides of the globe.

from the *Washington Post Fall Children's Books*
November 7, 1982

Sounds in the Heart

Several years ago I read an article about writing for children in which the writer said that her qualification for writing for children lay in her photographic memory. She had never forgotten anything that had happened to her as a child, and therefore she could write meaningfully for children. I have typically forgotten who the writer was and where the article appeared, and the only reason I remember the statement at all is that it made me resolve all over again not to read any more articles on the qualifications to be a writer for children.

Indeed, as I was writing *Jacob Have I Loved,* I was carrying on a running quarrel with Louise Bradshaw. I wanted to write the book in the third person because I knew perfectly well that no one—well, no one I knew—could remember her past in the kind of detail that Louise was pretending to. I was very nervous about this since I know I have a poor memory for specific events. When I am called upon to tell about something from my past, I find myself wondering in midstory how much of what I seem to be remembering actually occurred. Gilly Hopkins would probably say that I lie a lot, but I assure you that I do not lie intentionally. I seem, however, incapable of separating the bare facts from my constantly enlarging perception of those facts. It is part of what makes me a writer of fiction, for a writer of fiction is never content with mere fact; she must somehow find a pattern, a meaning in events.

Of course, this is what Louise Bradshaw has done from the vantage point of age. She has scooped out a hunk of her youth and molded it into a story. The difference between writing a story and simply relating past events is that a story, in order to be acceptable, must have shape and meaning. It is the old idea that art is the bringing of order out of chaos, and it is interesting to me how much I crave that order. Recently, I read Elizabeth Hardwick's *Sleepless Nights.* On the front of the jacket it is called a novel. On the back, it is called "subtle, beautiful, extraordinary, haunting, daring, miraculous, and almost perfect." For a change, I have little argument with the back of the book. It may very well be subtle, beautiful, extraordinary, haunting, daring, miraculous, and almost perfect. But it ain't no novel. At least it is not what I would ever call a novel. Perhaps there is order in the book, but if there is, it is far too subtle for me. I find no shape to the memories set down in this book, and I put it down deeply dissatisfied.

I believe it is the job of the novelist to shape human experience so that a reader might be able to find not only order but meaning in the story. It also seems to me that the way a writer shapes human experience depends to a great extent on her history—all those forces, most of which she had nothing to do with, that made her what she is. In speaking of those forces, we are speaking of our human heritage, our particular family history, and our individual past experience. These are the memories that we call up consciously or unconsciously as we write.

Among the many Chinese and Japanese ideographs for our word *idea* is one that combines the character for *sound* with the character for *heart*—the heart being the seat of the intelligence as well as of emotion. Thus, an idea is something that makes a sound in the heart. Now, if you want to change *idea* into a verb that means "to remember," you do so by adding an extra symbol for *heart.* In preparing to talk of the relation of memory to writing, I tried to ask myself as objectively as I could: What are the sounds that I hear in my deepest heart? What causes me to shape human experience in the way that I do?

If I tell you that I was born in China of Southern Presbyterian missionary parents, I have already given away the three chief clues to my tribal memory.

Let me start at the end and work backward through the description. Missionary parents. I have discovered as I have gone out into the world that most people do not regard missionary work as a respectable occupation. And I'm sure that many of us "mish kids" would argue whether having been born one was a plus or minus for the living of this life. There is no way to escape a certain peculiarity of personality. But all that comes later. For the most basic and most lasting gift of this parentage was a total identification with the children of Israel. The stories of the Bible were read to us not to make us good but to tell us who we were. It seems a bit strange to me, as I look back, that my feeling of kinship was not with the early Christian church but with the Hebrew people. In fact, it was years later, after considerable study of Paul's Epistles, that I had to come to the conclusion that *gentile* after all was not a dirty word.

It is still hard for me to accept as fact that my blood ancestors were gentiles and were until fairly recently painting themselves blue and running around naked. My real ancestors left Ur of the Chaldees with Abraham and wandered in the wilderness with Moses. Add to this strong biblical heritage its interpretation by Calvin, Knox, and the Westminster divines, and you have got one sure foundation beneath your feet. Again, it was amazing to me to learn that to most people Calvinism seems more like the foundation that ladies of my mother's generation used to wear—squeezing all the breath out of you and poking into you every step you took. This, of course, was not my experience. For if the Bible told me who I was, my Presbyterian tradition told me why I was.

"What is the chief end of man?" the Westminster catechism asks in its very first question; and we could all answer before we could read: "Man's chief end is to glorify God and enjoy him forever." Again, many people outside this tradition have a very different view of the Calvinist position. They think of it more like a slogan that was on a T-shirt our son John used to own. This one had four monkeys: Hear No Evil, See No Evil, Speak No Evil, Have No Fun. Other people contend to the contrary that Presbyterians see nothing but evil—from original sin to total depravity—dragging guilt through the world as Marley's ghost dragged his chains.

Still others can't understand why Presbyterians, who profess to believe in divine predestination in which everything depends on God, spend their lives working as if everything depended on them. I haven't the time, and you haven't the patience for me to pursue this line of thought in much more detail, but I bring it up because I am trying to discover what this heritage has to do with what I write.

The other day someone was telling me of an article he had read about a recent discovery of galaxies ten billion light-years from Earth, and it reminded me of something a former theology professor of mine said last year. He had just survived a heart attack and bypass surgery. "People are always asking me if I believe in the next world. Why," he said, "I can hardly believe in this one."

Those of us, you see, who were raised in this tradition know how puny we are. It is not our ability to understand or believe or remember that ultimately matters. That will come and go. But the truth we have drunk in with our mother's milk is that the one who flung the stars in their courses does not forget his children. A friend asked me how I dared to go into Louise's loss of faith. Wasn't I afraid that I would lose my own along the way? But I know that I am always carrying about within myself faith and unfaith, obedience and rebellion, trust and fear. When I write with the eyes of hope, it is not my own ability to believe that I am writing about but the biblical affirmation that God is faithful —justice and righteousness will prevail. In the words of one of my spiritual fathers, the Roman Catholic priest and poet Gerard Manley Hopkins: "Because the Holy Ghost over the bent / World broods with warm breast and with ah! bright wings."[1]

I am also a child of another heritage that will seem strange to most of you. Let me illustrate. A man I met at a party had just taken his son to Gettysburg and had found out a fascinating detail of history there. He learned, while at the site of Pickett's Charge, that the Union officer who had repulsed the charge and therefore saved the day and perhaps the Union was George Custer. "So, you see," he said, "Custer did have his moment of glory."

Now, this story did not have the effect he intended. The teller did not realize that I had been raised on the story of my grandfather's two older brothers who died in the War Between the States. (We even called the war by a different name where I came from.) One of these brothers was a cavalry officer under Pickett and was mortally wounded in that desperate, heroic charge. (Here again, those with a different heritage might call it suicidal or insane.)

There is a very romantic (once more from our point of view) story connected with my uncle's death. As he lay dying, a young Union chaplain came to him and asked if there was anything he could do. My uncle asked him to unpin the Confederate flags and cut two brass buttons from his uniform and send them to his father and his sweetheart in Georgia. He was able to tell the chaplain his name—Goetchius—but he died before he could give the chaplain his address. For years the chaplain carried the flags and buttons in his pocket, unable to forget the dying man's request but unable to fulfill it. Twenty years later, he was traveling on a ferryboat in Georgia and heard one of the black ferrymen address an elderly passenger as Marse Goetchius. He approached the man and asked him if he had had a relative who took part in Pickett's Charge. The man was my great-grandfather, whose son had been listed as missing in action all those years. Together he and the chaplain traveled to Pennsylvania. They located the trench grave because the corn grew taller and greener along it, and—as I was told as a child—they identified my uncle's body by his dental work. My great-grandfather took his son's remains home to Georgia. My mother remembered my uncle's sweetheart, who was, of course, no longer young when my mother knew her. She always reminded my mother and her sisters that she should have been their aunt. She never married and, I was told, treasured those two brass buttons until she died.

Now it doesn't matter that I know it would have been tragic if our nation had become two nations, one slave and one free. It doesn't matter that I think that the holding of slaves is an abomination before God and that to regard any other human being as inferior to oneself is a grievous sin. Somehow, there is still something in me that sees the glory in my uncle's death and not in Custer's triumph. The image of the saintly, larger-than-life Robert E. Lee in defeat will forever seem more magnificent than that of Ulysses S. What's-his-name in victory.

One of the things I was told as a child never to forget, and haven't, is that I have been kissed by Maude Henderson. (In my own defense, I should like to have it in the record that I spent an enormous effort in my childhood wriggling out from under kisses. Missionary children are fair game for any maudlin matron.) The significance of this particular kiss, however, is that when Maude Henderson was a little girl, her father, one of the landed Virginia gentry, was a close friend of Robert E. Lee's and a fellow vestryman in the Episcopal church in Lexington. The general used to give

little Maude rides on his horse. (I was sure that meant Trav-
eller, but I have no proof for those of you who prefer your
history straight.) Coming home together from a vestry meeting one evening, the general stopped by the Hendersons'
house to speak to his friend's wife, and as he was leaving,
he stooped and gave little Maude a kiss. Then he went home,
sat down at his own supper table, and slipped into uncon-
sciousness. Miss Maude explained to us that the general's
widow had told her that she must always remember that
although many people had kissed the general before he
died, she was the last person on earth whom *he* had kissed.
And my brother and sisters and I were to remember that she
in turn had kissed us. This would be even sappier than it
sounds (if that is possible), except that Maude Henderson is
one of the genuine heroes of my life. But more about her
later.

I want to make one probably obvious point about this
part of my heritage, which is that since 1865 we white
Southerners have been suckers for a losing cause. Struggle
dashed to defeat by inexorable might is somehow more glo-
rious than mere success. I, for example, cannot escape the
notion that those seven years when I was writing doggedly
and publishing nothing were far more honorable than the
years since. This heritage explains, of course, why I was
drawn to the Heike Clan rather than to the Genji when I read
Japanese history. And then, too, the Japanese tend to roman-
ticize the person who struggles but is in the end brought
down.

This brings me to the third sound in my heart—the music
of the East. Among my earliest memories are those of a
Chinese woman who lived very close to us. When I was four

years old, it was my habit every day to walk to Mrs. Loo's house precisely at her lunchtime. One day as I was going out on my usual jaunt, my mother said to me in what I'm sure she thought was a joking manner, "If you keep on eating so much Chinese food, you might turn into a little Chinese girl." Her remark bothered me. I didn't really want to give up the parents I had. But it didn't bother me enough to keep me from going to Mrs. Loo's for lunch. Today, I still discover that when I am happy and want to celebrate, I will cook Japanese food; but when I hit bottom and need all the comfort life can afford, it is Chinese food that I crave. This is a very physical heritage of smell and sight and touch, because these are my earliest impressions.

Chinese was my first language, although I quickly became bilingual. When I was five, we were refugeed to the United States for the first time, and even though we returned to China the following year, only my father got back to our home in Hwaian. The rest of us lived among foreigners, so my fluency in Chinese disappeared. I have forgotten Chinese almost entirely, but I believe and hope it is still there, bred into my bones along with steamed pork dumplings.

I spend a lot of time trying to explain to people that China and Japan are two different countries with different languages, histories, and cultures, although I cannot but feel that those early years in China prepared me in a unique way to live in Japan.

My father was raised a farmer in the Shenandoah Valley of Virginia. His people never owned slaves, although they were farming the valley before the revolutionary war. They were a combination of German peasant and Scotch-Irish rock, fiercely independent, glorying in God and in their own strong backs. My father went from Washington and Lee University to join the French as an ambulance driver before the United States entered World War I. He left his right leg in France and brought home a croix de guerre and a dose of toxic gas. He was, I believe, as ideally suited as any Westerner to go to China. He was intelligent, hard-working, almost fearless, absolutely stoical, and amazingly humble, with the same wonderful sense of humor found in many Chinese. Not only was he capable of learning the language and enduring the hardships of his chosen life, but also he was incapable of seeing himself in the role of Great White Deliverer.

We lived, unlike most foreigners of that era, in a Chinese house in a school complex where all of our neighbors were Chinese. My father's coworker and closest friend was the first son of a first son, a well-born man, and a recognized scholar. He chose to become a Christian pastor. He and my father traveled together, riding donkeys from village to village, sleeping on the straw in flea-ridden pigsties because they were the best accommodations some friendly farmers could offer. Where there was famine—as there too often was—they went with food, and where there was plague or disease, they went with medicine. Mr. Lee disappeared in the first Communist purges in 1949, and my father grieved for him until he died.

What this meant for me was that when I went to Japan many years later, I had, through no virtue of my own, an attitude toward the Orient that most Westerners, especially the Americans I met there, seemed to lack. I knew that I had come to a civilization far older than my own, to a language that after a lifetime of study I would still be just beginning to grasp, to a people whose sense of beauty I could only hope to appreciate but never to duplicate.

Against these convictions, there was, of course, a fear. The only Japanese I had known as a child were enemy soldiers. What made it possible for me to go to Japan at all was a close friend I had in graduate school, a Japanese woman pastor who persuaded me that despite the war I would find a home in Japan if I would give the Japanese people a chance. And she was right. In the course of four years I was set fully free from my deep, childish hatred. I truly loved Japan, and one of the most heartwarming compliments I ever received came from a Japanese man I worked with who said to me one day that someone had told him that I had been born in China. Was that true? I assured him it was. "I knew it," he said. "I've always known there was something Oriental about you."

How, then, has this affected how and what I write? The setting of my first three novels is the most obvious result. But there are other things, some of which I can identify and some which I cannot. One thing living in Japan did for me was to make me feel that what is left out of a work of art is as important as, if not more important than, what is put in. (As Virginia Buckley, my editor, will testify, I tend from time to time to eliminate to the point of obscurity, but the principle is a good one.) I am also a great lover of form. As a writer, I seek freedom within a form. I rather doubt that I am capable of truly experimental art. And form for me has something to do with the order woven into the universe.

A friend of mine who had lived in Japan for a number of years was preparing to return to the States, and at her farewell party a young student said to her, "You must tell them the truth about us." "What do you want me to say?" she asked. "Tell them that we have four seasons," he replied. Now, if you know anything about the Japanese, you know that this is not an idle request. The sound that rings deepest in the Japanese heart is not Sony or Mitsubishi or even Honda, but spring, summer, fall, or winter. Every time I change the season in a novel, I remember that I have lived in this rhythm. I have known the glory of spring as seen in the cherry blossoms, which so quickly fade and fall to the earth, reminding us that life, too, is fleeting but that the seasons continue, the earth turns, and an order greater than our single lives prevails.

As I was trying somehow to pull together this talk, it came to revolve, to my surprise, around Maude Henderson, the woman who as a little girl had been kissed by Robert E. Lee. The reason I knew Maude Henderson was not because she came from Lexington, Virginia, where my father's people have lived for more than two hundred years. Her family was wealthy and Episcopalian; mine was solvent and Presbyterian. Maude Henderson and my parents became friends in Shanghai. Miss Maude left her elegant Virginia home to become a deaconess in the Episcopal church. She went out to China at about the turn of the century, and there, in the poorest section of Shanghai, she opened a home for abandoned baby girls. She was their mother in every way and stayed in that home for forty-nine years. Her teeth fell out, as did most of her hair. When Japanese soldiers pillaging the city appeared at her door, demanding her girls, she stood there, all of five feet tall, and would not move. They would have to kill her first, she said. They didn't kill her. Even after December 1941, when they were arresting all

Americans and determined that she must be arrested, they made it house arrest—her own house, with her current generation of girls.

In 1949 she was forced out of China, and for the first time in fifty years she came back to Virginia. We were living in West Virginia at the time, and she got on a bus and came to see us. My mother was a wonderful cook, and Miss Maude loved every bite. "I've only got one tooth left," she told us, "but it's all right. The doctor says it's my sweet one." She had then only the barest suggestion of white hair under her deaconess's cap, and her face looked exactly as though it had been shriveled like dried apple, but from deep among the wrinkles, her blue eyes shone with humor and delight. I find in Maude Henderson the convergence of all my heritages. I will never forget her. And the fact that she kissed me will sound and resound in my deepest heart.

Heart Strings
and Other Attachments

MIDNIGHT HOUR ENCORES

by Bruce Brooks

With his first book, *The Moves Make the Man,* Bruce Brooks
established himself as a master of the extended metaphor.
In that multiple-award-winning novel, basketball was the
dazzling language of life; now, before readers have really
caught their breath from that achievement, Brooks has
turned his considerable storytelling powers to the world
of music and the coming of age of a prodigy.

Sibilance T. Spooner plays both life and the cello with
"cunning and arrogance," two words which keep cropping
up in the reviews of her concerts. Sib (who also renamed
herself at the age of eight) has, from her own account, pretty
much raised herself. She lives in the District of Columbia
with Taxi her father, an exile from the '60s who edits an
environmental newsletter. In a wonderful introductory first
chapter, Sib tells how at nine, when all the other girls in her

class were in love with horses, she asks Taxi to show her a horse.

He puts her in the car, drives her to a camping area six hours from home, then gets her up at dawn and walks her to the top of an enormous sand dune.

"I suddenly notice that the pounding of the surf is getting louder from a specific direction, the way a secondary theme sneaks into melody from the violas in an orchestra. And when I look in that direction, off to my left, instead of surf I see a sudden wild spray of beautiful monster from Mars swirl out from behind a dune, gracefully rolling toward me, not snorting or shivering but just *running,* running on the flat beach beneath me, splashing in the edges of the tide and emptying those little pools with a single stroke of a hoof."

The remainder of the book unravels the mesh of feelings and history, personal and public, tangled in Sib's request at age sixteen that Taxi show her her mother.

Early on in the book, Sib compares books to music, and books lose because ". . . books are so damn locked up. To me, the little black words on a page are stiffer than steel forks, more closed than the stones in the Great Wall of China. . . . Music is different. Music is written down, but it's not stony and stiff—in fact, the guy who wrote it wants me to fool around with it a bit, to poke into the special places I discover, to set my own pace, to tell the story with my own accents."

The other two-hundred-odd pages of the book give a lie to that distinction. This is a book the reader will have to fool around with, poke into, and tell in his own accents. Brooks keeps you going on at least three lines of suspense, not including the question of whether, through all this, Sib will become a more likeable human being. And in the end, as you applaud the gesture which reveals her humanity, you are appalled by the cost of it. Then you remember the missing cello case and begin rewriting the ending to satisfy the accents of your own life.

I was reminded again of Holden Caulfield's definition of a good book as one that "when you're all done reading it, you wish the author that wrote it was a terrific friend of yours and you could call him up on the phone whenever you felt like it."

I want to call up Bruce Brooks and say that the trouble with a book so far ahead of the pack is that by page 15 I'm demanding it be perfect. So I notice Sib's abuse of "like" and "into" and Taxi's lapses into didacticism, and I want to quarrel about the ending, or at least make the author explain exactly what he was about, which he probably won't. But anyhow, while I have him on the line, I can tell him thanks for another terrific book.

from the *Washington Post Book World*
November 9, 1986

The Spying Heart

"Thoughts and Dreams: Touchstones in Time." As I was thinking about this talk today, I could not help but remember my distinguished colleagues who would be speaking here during this conference. What would there be left to say by Saturday morning? All the meaty words in the title would have been well digested before I ever stood up. I've heard a number of these people before. I know Jean Karl would have filled you all full of thoughts, and who could beat Jane Yolen at painting dreams? Charlotte Huck would have expertly preempted all the literary touchstones, and Eleanor Cameron has theories of time that boggle my mind. Well, I thought, that leaves me with the choice between a conjunction and a preposition. Then I remembered Eric Carle, who is concerned with transitions and would have taken care of any loose prepositions.

But don't worry, friends. It is perfectly all right. I'm very fond of conjunctions, especially the word *and.* As any careful grammarian reading my books will observe, I start a lot of my sentences with the word *and.* Not nearly as many as I would if I didn't have such a good editor, but certainly enough to scandalize my sixth-grade teacher. "You *never* begin a sentence with a conjunction," she would say. "A conjunction *connects* words, phrases, or clauses," thereby relegating, as she thought, a very humble role to the lowly conjunction. But Miss Lowrance (she always accented the second syllable) was wrong to downplay the conjunction. Connecting is a vital, not a minor function. Connecting is what you and I are primarily concerned with. That's what imagination is all about.

I think it was Karl Barth who said that he was more of a fundamentalist than the Fundamentalists, because he knew what was fundamental. I do not have the kind of certainty that Barth had. But I'm growing more and more to believe that our fundamental task as human beings is to seek out connections—to exercise our imaginations.

It follows, then, that the basic task of education is the care and feeding of the imagination. We used to know this. Indeed, the earliest form of education was the telling of stories. But nowadays stories have been relegated to the realm of the frivolous. Education has chosen to emphasize decoding and computation rather than the cultivation of the imagination. We like, you see, what we can manage. We can decide which year we're going to teach which fact, function, or word, and we can give a child a multiple-choice test at the end to see if he has got it. We want our

mathematics and our mythology strictly compartment-
alized, for we know instinctively that the imagination is a
wild, hardly tamable commodity. There is no way to measure it objectively, so anything in the curriculum that has to
do with the growth of the inner life of a child we tend to
classify as a frill and either shove it to the periphery or eliminate it from the curriculum altogether.

I remember my shock when I was taken on a tour of the
new school in our neighborhood. I saw the classrooms, the
gymnasium, the industrial arts class, the home economics
lab—"But," I protested, "it doesn't have any windows."
"Oh," said my guide, "studies have proven that if a
school has windows, students will waste a great deal of
time staring out of them." I didn't say anything, but I
know perfectly well that the only way I survived my public school education at all was the fact that there were windows through which I could stare out.

The growth of the imagination demands windows—windows through which we can look out at the world and windows through which we can look into ourselves. The old
stories were windows in just this way.

Now the serpent was more subtil than any beast of
the field which the Lord God had made. And he said
unto the woman, Yea, hath God said, Ye shall not eat
of every tree of the garden?

And the woman said unto the serpent, We may eat
of the fruit of the trees of the garden:

But of the fruit of the tree which is in the midst of
the garden, God hath said, Ye shall not eat of it, neither
shall ye touch it, lest ye die.

And the serpent said unto the woman, Ye shall not surely die:

For God doth know that in the day ye eat thereof, then your eyes shall be opened, and ye shall be as gods, knowing good and evil.[1]

I don't have to tell you the story—I just want to remind you that here the teller is giving us a window, not only into how evil entered the Garden of Paradise but into the human spirit.

The story gives us a language for the unknown. It shapes chaos for us and fills it with meaning. In tree and fruit and serpent, all of which we can picture concretely in the mind's eye, we can begin to deal with fearsome unseen forces. But in order to do this for us, the story must ring true. It must tell us something we already know but didn't realize we knew.

The old stories do this for us. If they didn't they wouldn't have lasted. But what about those of us who presume to write new stories? I can't speak for other writers, but there is something about me that makes other people want to help me with my work. Perfect strangers will come up to me and say, "Now, here's the book you ought to write." Or, "Let me tell you what your next book should be." Or, "I've got a story that's absolutely perfect for you." Contrary creature that I am, these perfect ideas for books never seem to suit me. They seem invariably to fall into two categories—exactly-like stories and role-model stories.

Now the exactly-like story proponents are people, young and old, who feel that today's readers won't read any stories unless they are written about people exactly like themselves. A friend of mine who is a librarian in a junior high school said to me once that she wished I hadn't given Gilly Hopkins a definite age. "What do you mean?" I asked. "Well," she answered, "if she weren't a specific age, more kids would be able to identify with her." Now my feeling is that there are certain givens in life. Everyone has a birthday, and a character without a birthday is not human or mortal. If Gilly had had no birthday, *no one* would have been able to identify with her because she would have been totally unreal. It is a fallacy that a child or young person cannot fully enjoy a book about a person of a different age or state. Otherwise *Millions of Cats* would never have sold millions of copies. Or how do you account for the popularity of *Charlotte's Web*? Surely our elementary school population is not divided into spiders on the one hand and pigs on the other.

In addition to the exactly-like school, there is the role-model school. I had a question last week from a really fine librarian in Virginia, asking me what had happened to all the good families in children's books. There just weren't any exemplary families these days. I racked my brain to find an exemplary family in children's literature of any day. There are, of course, the Marches, but they would never have gotten into a book if Papa had stayed home and made a living for his family instead of packing up for war. There are a few of us who read the Arthur Ransome books, but not many exemplary parents today would feel comfortable with giving their children the kind of freedom those children had. Let's face it: You can't have much of a story without adventure and conflict, and good parents are always getting in the way of both, especially when there are two of them around to back each other up.

If model parents tend to destroy a good tale, so do role-model characters. We may not want characters exactly like ourselves, but we do want believable people in our stories. Someone exactly like myself provides no window on a wider world, and someone who is too exemplary a role model fails to provide me with a connection. A book that comes from the writer's deepest imagination provides both a window and a connection.

Let me share with you part of an essay on writing fiction by Shirley Hazzard that appeared in the *New York Times Book Review.*

William Butler Yeats said that "if we understand our own minds, and the things that are striving to utter themselves through our minds, we move others, not because we have thought about those others, but because all life has the same root." Through art, as in dreams, we can experience this truth, this root of life, as Yeats calls it. Through art, we can respond ideally to truth as we cannot in life. To suggest the nature of that truth—which is the writer's material—I should like to go outside literature for a moment and draw on the view of a painter—Veronese, who in 1572 was called before the Holy Office at Venice to explain why, in a painting of the Last Supper, he had included figures of loiterers, passersby, people scratching themselves, deformed people, a man having a nosebleed, and so on: details then held unfit to appear in a holy subject. When this grave charge of blasphemy was pressed on Veronese by the examiners, who asked him why he had shown such profane matters in a holy picture, he replied, "I thought these things might happen."

Despite the many convoluted theories expended on the novelist's material, its essence is in those words.[2]

"I thought these things might happen." The Sino-Japanese character pronounced *so,* which means "to imagine," has three parts. First you draw a tree and then you draw an eye behind that tree. And then, underneath the eye spying out from behind the tree, you put a heart. Go to work on that for a minute. I love the idea of spying as tied up with the act of imagining. And since the heart in Japanese is the seat both of feeling and of the intellect, we're not talking about some sentimental peeping, but the kind of spying, the kind of connecting that Einstein did, and Shakespeare, and Gerard Manley Hopkins.

And what of *image*? We've trivialized the word beyond recognition. We say, "What image do you wish to project?" Well, if you want to look the successful career woman, you can buy books that will tell you how to do it, so with X number of dollars, you can project the proper image. It doesn't matter so much what you are, but what you look like. More soberly, we are told in the United States today that it matters not at all what a politician stands for, only what image he projects on television. Image is thus style, not substance.

But I want to go back to a more basic definition of image —image as real likeness. The image of God is not God, but it is a likeness, a real entity in itself. It is not simply a shadow; it is capable of casting its own shadow. This takes us back to the realm of those archetypes in the barely explored regions of the human mind that, when imagination comes into play, we find ourselves sharing in a mysterious joining of minds through the history of the human race. The old stories—when no one has scrubbed them up—take us to these most basic images. Perhaps, indirectly, all real stories do.

A teacher friend was telling me the other day of trying to teach her literature class about imagery. She was trying to make the point that imagery is concrete. As she was talking, I began trying to recall what the Sino-Japanese character for *image* was. Since I am not blessed with a photographic or even a particularly good memory, I was forced to wait until I got home to look it up. There it was—*image*—or *zo*—made up of two other words—the one on the left the character for *person* and the one on the right the character for *elephant.* Elephant? I gave a short sigh for the loss of elegance and then comforted myself that the Chinese and the Japanese, too, knew that an image must have substance, there being few things more substantial than an elephant. But even so, why an elephant? Back when the character was invented they didn't even have elephants in China—at least I don't think they did. Maybe the word *zo* stood for a sort of mythical beast, a leviathan of the land. Then suddenly one day someone came over the Burmese mountains riding an elephant and a Chinese said, "As I live and breathe, a real, live *zo.*"

You see what comes from spending your childhood looking out of school windows.

Anyhow, if you want to write the word *imagination* in Japanese, you begin with *so*—the word for "to imagine," which has the eye spying out from behind a tree over a heart—and then add *zo*—which is "the person beside the elephant." *Sozo*—the spying heart and the concrete image.

We need to recall this when we try to help children to develop their imaginations. So often we demand creativity out of the blue. We ask them simply to express themselves, and when they flounder in this impossible task, we blame TV and arcade games for robbing them of their God-given imaginations. Now, it occurs to me that perhaps people don't have much in the way of imagination to start with. We may have images buried deep inside, but the imaging, the imagining, the spying of the heart—the deep connection of those images that comprise the inner life with corresponding images in the world outside ourselves—and the language or the artistic skill with which to express this connection—these are what must grow and develop.

We start this process of nurturing the imagination when we read to children while they are still far too young to understand the words. We read them the old stories, of course, but we also share with them other works of the imagination. A child who is struggling with all the wild things within himself sits snuggled close to his mother as she reads *Where the Wild Things Are* and is deeply comforted. Even though his wild self may sail across the seas, he can come home again to where his supper is waiting—still hot. An older child facing the same struggle—and it is a lifetime job —finds the images she needs in *The Wizard of Earthsea.* I do believe that the climactic scene where Ged finally goes forth to meet the terrible shadow from which he has so long fled —I do believe that this is one of the most powerful scenes I have ever read in any book. My daughter agrees.

Last year I was speaking at a conference at the University of Kentucky. They wrote me and said that in addition to my talk, they were planning to have a panel, two psychiatrists and a social worker, to discuss the use of books with troubled children. Would I like to be part of the panel? No thank you, I said. I'm always terrified by talk of using books. I'm so concerned that the reader be free to come to a book from his own experience and take from the book what he can and will. I don't want anyone telling a child what he should get out of one of my books or any book I care about, for that matter. Anyhow, although I declined to be on the panel, I did sit at the back of the room and listen. It was a deeply moving experience to listen to three highly competent, obviously compassionate people tell about the healing power of the imagination. They never diagnosed a child and then prescribed a particular book. They read widely themselves and had available in their offices many books. "When I get to know a child," one of them said, "I also know four or five books that I think he might like and that might mean something to him. I say, 'Here are some books I've liked that I thought you might like. Would you like to borrow one of them?' The child always makes his own selection. There is no suggestion that he is to report to me what he has learned. If he doesn't like a book, either because it doesn't speak to him or speaks too threateningly for him to listen, he simply stops reading. And that's fine. One of the basic tenets of therapy is readiness. A patient simply rejects an idea if he is not ready for it. But I have seen books that have a very powerful healing effect. For example, handicapped young people often spend most of their lives trying to conceal their handicaps. When a young person like that reads *The Wizard of Earthsea,* it can be a very liberating experience."

I cannot believe that when Ursula Le Guin conceived the idea for *The Wizard of Earthsea* she had in mind an epileptic teenager. But because all of life has the same root, her fantasy of a novice wizard in an unknown world plunges the reader to his or her own emotional and imaginative roots and makes connections the author herself wouldn't have dreamed of.

I'd like to share with you a story that came in a letter from a woman who owns a children's bookstore in New Mexico. It has to do with a book I did not write, but that I did have the privilege of translating from Japanese into English.

"This is what happened," the bookseller said in her letter to me, "when I got my single solitary copy of *The Crane Wife.*

"It came all by itself, like a dust devil. I opened it up and put it on the desk, meaning to take it home and read it, but my three-year-old, who goes to work with me every day, insisted that we read it. So I did, while a customer was browsing, quite unattended. I was reduced to pitiful tears for a long while. Matthew was quite affected, too. We put the copy back on the shelf of new books and looked at it suspiciously all day long.

"Next day, first thing, in came a lady about forty years old, carrying a lovely little two-year-old girl. She was dressed in white tights, black patent leather Mary Janes, and a Polly Flinders dress.

"The lady said, 'This little girl needs a book about death.' [This was sort of her everyday line of business, so the request was not too far out, explained the bookseller parenthetically.]

"I replied, 'Give me a clue. Was it a dog or a cat or a grandmother?'

" 'No, her father shot her mother and then shot himself.' "

Yes, friends, I had exactly the same reaction when I first read the bookseller's letter as you are having to the story as I repeat it. To our knowledge, no one has ever written a book for a two-year-old child whose father has murdered her mother and then killed himself. Even if such a book had been written, I cannot imagine that it would have been published or that any of you would have purchased it. There are no how-to's for human tragedy. There are, however, works of the imagination that can minister to human lives in mysterious ways. The bookseller who wrote me said that while she was standing in shocked silence mentally rejecting one book on death after another, her son said, "What about *The Crane Wife*?"

"I had my doubts," she continued, "what with the blood scene and all. But the lady took it. She came back later in the week and told me that it had indeed helped smooth over the lumps, to open up the tears, to let the child identify with a concept alien to toddlers.

"Thank you for *The Crane Wife.* Why it came when it did, and why I read it to Matthew when I did, and why he thought of it when he did, are all beyond my ken. But thank you anyway, from us all."

Thanks are in order, but not to me. Though, unlike three-year-old Matthew, I would never have thought to offer this book to a two-year-old at all, much less one in such a situation, I chose to translate this book because of the power of its imaginative vision. And although I would not have been wise enough to offer this book, I can see in retrospect the sadness of the story brought to life in its exquisite pictures that would take a child's grief with utter seriousness and the beauty that would enfold and bear her up. To show you how different readers take from the same story quite different visions, I want to share with you something of the meaning *The Crane Wife* has for me. The wounded crane who comes back in the form of a young woman sets up a loom and closes it off with sliding paper doors. Then she says to her simple country husband, "Please, I beg you, I beg you never look in upon me while I am weaving."

The effort of weaving seems to exhaust the young woman, yet the fabric she weaves has an unearthly beauty, and her poor husband can sell it at a great price. But, as time goes by, he becomes greedy and consumed with curiosity when he is exiled to the other side of the sliding doors.

Tonkara tonkara. The sound of the loom continued on and on into the fifth day. The work in the back room seemed to be taking longer than ever.

Yohei, no longer the simple fellow that he had once

been, began to wonder about certain peculiar things. Why did the young woman appear to grow thinner every time she wove? What was going on in there behind those paper doors? How could she weave such beautiful cloth when she never seemed to buy any thread?

The longer he had to wait, the more he yearned to peep into the room until, at last, he put his hand upon the door.

"Ah!" came a voice from within. At the same time Yohei cried out in horror and fell back from the doorway.

What Yohei saw was not human. It was a crane, smeared with blood, for with its beak it had plucked out its own feathers to place them in the loom.[3]

Ah, I thought, when I read this. That is what art is all about. It is weaving fabric from the feathers you have plucked from your own breast. But no one must ever see the process—only the finished bolt of goods. They must never suspect that that crimson thread running through the pattern is blood. I must stop analyzing and talking about the process, I said. I've got to keep those paper doors shut. And so I should, but not because critics or reviewers or readers are nosy outsiders who have no right to peer in. No. The rude fellow with a hand on the door is myself. When she sets out to spin a story, the spying heart is involved in a fragile magic. I must trust the weaver of thoughts and dreams within and leave her to work as she will. Reason and greed and impatience and curiosity must be kept in check. Else someday I may wake up and find the crane wife has flown away.

Family Visions

SWEET WHISPERS, BROTHER RUSH
by Virginia Hamilton

"The first time Teresa saw Broth was the way she would think of him ever after. Tree fell head over heels for him. It was love at first sight in a wild beating of her heart that took her breath. But it was a dark Friday three weeks later when it rained, hard and wicked, before she knew Brother Rush was a ghost."

This is the first paragraph of Virginia Hamilton's new book. The last time a first paragraph chilled my spine like this one, I was sixteen years old, hunched over a copy of *Rebecca.* There are those who say that Virginia Hamilton is a great writer but that her books are hard to get into. This one is not. It fairly reaches off the first page to grab you, and once it's got you, it sets you spinning deeper and deeper into its story. Needless to say, this is not a conventional ghost story. In fact, the function of the ghost in this book, like that of the pole in *M. C. Higgins the Great,* is to provide fourteen-year-old Tree Pratt with a place from which to view her world.

When the story opens, Tree's world consists of a ghetto school and a city apartment in which she lives with her slightly retarded older brother, Dabney. Their father disappeared before Tree can remember. Their mother is a practical nurse who lives where she works, reappearing on the odd weekend to give them money and buy groceries. The children never know when she will come home or quite how to reach her in the meantime. The only other regular in their lives is an old bag lady who comes in to clean on Saturdays and who is so poor and weak that she spends most of the day resting and eating Tree and Dab's food supply.

At first Brother Rush lingers at the edge of Tree's life. She sees him on the street in his dark pin-stripe suit, ivory shirt, silver buckle with "Jazz" spelled out in fancy script, dress shoes, and gray silk socks. He is light-years beyond the other street dudes and becomes the object of her adolescent yearnings. One rainy day she goes into a tiny room where she can be alone to draw and think, and she finds that Brother Rush has come "smack through the hard wood of the round table of the little room. She knew all right:

"Be a damned ghost."

Brother Rush has one hand cupped to his ear as though listening for something. What is he listening for? Then he holds out to Tree a space shaped like an oval mirror through which Tree is drawn into the world of her babyhood, unable for a time to determine whether she is mother or child.

Through the space of Brother Rush, Tree mystically learns the tragic history of her mother's people. But why does she need to know these things? Why has Brother Rush come? What are his whispers—the message—that he will not give directly but that Tree must discover for herself? In the end it seems that Brother's red Buick is the sweet chariot of death come to carry her brother home and leave Tree behind in a strange, wide world where she must learn to accept help and to offer forgiveness.

The supernatural, the search for identity, the need to belong to a family and the pain of belonging, the encounter with death—Miss Hamilton has taken ideas that occur repeatedly in books for the young and bathed them in her unique black light. Her readers have come to expect stories peopled with almost mythic black characters, but in this book everyone we meet, including the ghost, is wonderfully human: Tree, in the depths of her grief, takes secret delight in the attentions of a young man; her mother, Vy, who, when young, abused her strange little boy, is able as a woman to care for him with efficiency and love but still cannot call him by his name; and Miss Cenithia Pricherd, in her pageboy wig, is the prickliest, most lovable bag lady you'd ever want to know. The language too is of Miss Hamilton's own special kind, which uses the speech forms of the young to enhance rather than restrict the music of the book.

There is no need for me to say anything to those fierce Hamilton fans who will leap joyfully into anything she writes. But to the more timid reader, young or old, who may feel inadequate to Miss Hamilton's always demanding fiction, I say: Just read the first page, just the first paragraph, of *Sweet Whispers, Brother Rush.* Then stop—if you can.

from the *New York Times Book Review*
November 14, 1982

Why?

There is a question that I get everywhere I go these days. The question is, Why do you write for children? Although it's a question I'm constantly being asked, it is one for which I have never had an adequate response. Perhaps, I thought, if I write a speech about it, I might figure out for myself why I write for children.

But it's not easy to begin. You see, I not only don't know why I write for children, I don't know why I became a writer at all. I never meant to be a writer. When budding young novelists of ten or eleven ask me, "When did you first know that you wanted to be a writer?" I feel rather embarrassed to admit that I was already a writer and well past my thirtieth birthday before I realized that a writer was indeed what I wanted to be when I grew up.

I wrote as a child but I certainly didn't plan to be a writer. I loved books, and I read a great deal, but I never imagined that I might write them. Actually, when I was nine, I had a dual fantasy life in which on some days I was the leader of a group of commandos saving the world from Axis domination, and on others I was the benevolent queen of the United States of America. Of course, I indulged in these grandiose fantasies because I was finding the real world a tough place to inhabit.

Once, over lunch with another children's writer, we found ourselves exchanging schooldays horror stories. But, unlike me, Beth was a gutsy little kid. She fought back. She wrote to Ann Landers complaining about her sixth-grade teacher. When the teacher went into her desk, found the letter, opened the sealed and stamped envelope, and read it, Beth dragged her down to the principal's office on the charge of interfering with the U.S. mails, which eleven-year-old Beth knew to be a federal offense. And do you know what the principal said? To the teacher, mind you? "You are out of line."

I loved it. If I'd had sense enough to fantasize that scene it would have beaten out the royal pretensions and military triumphs in nothing flat.

"Why do you write children's books?" I asked her. "You don't have any childhood problems that need working out. You did it on the spot."

Well, there, I've let it slip. Yes, I probably do still have lots of childhood goblins that need exorcising. How could I ever deny the connection between James Johnson's troubled life at General Douglas MacArthur Elementary School and certain bleak days in my own past?

Why?

I worry about Mr. Dolman a lot. I, too, have been a teacher. And I know, with the rarest of exceptions, that teachers do not see with the eyes of a child. I still remember a child I taught once and wonder if he thought of me the way James thinks of Mr. Dolman. I didn't intend to humiliate him. I was just trying to jog him to be a little more responsible. It is not a memory I wish to dwell upon.

Now that I have been a parent and a writer as well as a child, I seem always to be on the child's side. But I know that children are not fair. They do not see either their teachers or their parents objectively. They only see from their own limited vision. When I write for children I try not only to be true to a child's point of view but I try as well to give hints that the world is wider than it seems to a child, and that other people may be more complex and even more understanding and compassionate than the child character sees them to be.

For a writer to succeed in this attempt, however, demands the cooperation of a careful and perceptive reader. There are those who think that a writer for children should not ask for this level of wisdom from her readers. Maybe not. But I don't seem able to write in any other way, and I have been very fortunate in the readers who choose my books. A great number of them seem not only willing to dig below the surface, they seem eager to. "I didn't catch on the first time I read it, but when I read it again . . ." is a refrain I hear surprisingly often. And, I must say, it is music to a writer's ears.

Why do you write for children? In the past year, I've begun to answer the question defensively. When someone asks "Why?" my response has been "Why not?" Because it has begun to occur to me that it is the implied objection that needs defending, not my choice of audience.

Why not write for children? If I became a writer for children more or less accidentally, I soon learned that I had stumbled into what was for me the world's best job—perhaps, as I say to my husband, the only job I'd be able to keep.

Any free-lance writer has the opportunity of choosing her own subjects and her own work methods and schedule, but I, as a writer for children, have an even more enviable situation. I know when I spend a year, two years, or more on a book, that I will be sending it to people who value books. Their first question is not, "How can we turn this manuscript into a property that will make money for us?" but, "How can we turn this manuscript into a book that children will want to read?"

I know that the book I have written will be carefully, even lovingly edited and copyedited. If a book is to have illustrations, I know that a lot of thought will be given to selecting an appropriate illustrator. Whether the book is illustrated or not, a designer will make sure that its look will be satisfying. I have had books where jacket illustration after jacket illustration was rejected because it didn't reflect what my editor felt was the heart of the story. Other houses may have different philosophies, but at the houses where I have been fortunate enough to work, it is the book itself that is of primary importance, not any subsidiary sales that it might eventually bring to the publisher.

My publishing houses have known that it takes time for a children's book to find its readers, and they are willing to keep a book in print long enough for that to happen. I have friends who write novels for adults who find their books on a remainder table in less than six months of their original publication. An adult novel is declared a best-seller before it is published by dint of advertising dollars and pre-publication sales to chain bookstores and paperback and movie contracts. A child's book becomes a best-seller because it is read and loved by hundreds of thousands of children who literally wear out the originally published copies.

Still, people seem to think that a writer who is any good at all is wasting her efforts writing exclusively for children. "No one will ever take you seriously," I'm told by speakers who do not even realize that they have just relegated to nonpersonhood not only me but all the children who read my books and take them quite seriously. But that's because in this country we refuse to take children seriously.

In 1981 I was invited to the Polish Embassy, and the ambassador awarded me a medal presented to *Bridge to Terabithia* by the Polish section of the International Board on Books for Young People in honor of Janusz Korczak.

"I need to explain to you about this man," the ambassador said. And during the informal ceremony in the embassy parlor he talked of Korczak, who was one of the first people in Europe to be concerned about the nurture, education, and psychology of children. He was a director of two orphanages in the city of Warsaw—one Jewish, the other gentile. When the Germans invaded he was given a chance to escape the country, but he chose to move into the ghetto with his Jewish orphans, and when they were taken to Treblinka, he went with them. At the train station, he took two children by the hand. The rest followed him, heads held high, into the boxcar. It is told that the guards from the ghetto saluted as he passed.

"I cannot claim," the ambassador went on, "that my father and Dr. Korczak were friends, but my father, too, taught pedagogy at the University of Warsaw, so they were colleagues. And since my father also died violently during the occupation, I always think of them together."

In November 1981, Poland was in turmoil. There were food riots in Warsaw on the same day that I was given the medal and had a leisurely lunch with the ambassador. Three weeks later, Ambassador Spasowski resigned his post and defected in order, he said, "to show my solidarity with the Polish people." I suppose that awarding that medal honoring a children's psychologist and protector to a writer of a book for children was among his last official acts.

I'll never forget that day. Nor will I forget the commentary on it made by a friend of mine. "What other country do you know of," she asked, "that has for a hero someone who gave his life for children?"

You see, we are not accustomed to taking children that seriously. That's why we call a school lunch program a frill and weapons, necessities. That's why we can mortgage our children's future with an unbelievable deficit and casually poison the environment in which they will have to live.

Can you begin to imagine the difference it would make to the present and to the future of the world if we were to begin to take children seriously? For one thing, we would respect the adults who care for and educate children. At the very least we would make sure they were carefully selected, rigorously trained, and generously compensated.

I don't need to tell you how far from the real world such

fantasies are, but at least those of us who do take children
seriously should stop apologizing for what we do. "I am only
a teacher." "I am only a librarian." "I am only a mother." "I
only write for children." We've let the rest of our society sell
us cheap. And in so doing we've betrayed the children entrusted to our care and nurture.

The scientist Jacob Bronowski was one of those rare people who take children seriously. The final chapter of his
book *The Ascent of Man* is titled "The Long Childhood." Bronowski argued that it is our long childhood that has made
us not only unique in nature but that has allowed us to
develop civilization. For most of human history, you see,
there was no distinct period called childhood. In the nomad
tribes of Persia, for example, the girls are already little mothers and the boys little herdsmen. What distinguishes no-
madic life from what we consider civilization is the long
childhood. The time and opportunity for the young to learn
not only how to imitate the parent—animals do that—but a
time for the child to develop strategies for life, values to live
by.

Looking at the great civilizations of China, India, and
Europe in the Middle Ages, Bronowski declares that by one
test they all fail: "They limit the freedom of the imagination
of the young."[1]

And what of us? We have been willing to risk bankruptcy
of the wealthiest nation in the world to build weapons of
mass destruction, but we have pled poverty when it comes
to nurturing the imaginations of our young. We don't have
the money to buy books, we don't have the money for
breakfasts or lunches that will fuel their brains as well as
their bodies. "A mind is a terrible thing to waste," an ad for

The United Negro College Fund tells us, but we continue to do so because we don't take children seriously.

But maybe it's more than that. Perhaps we are afraid of what might happen should the young truly begin to think. We've seen it in history over and over. Socrates in Athens, Sir Thomas More in England, Janusz Korczak in Warsaw, Gandhi in India, Jesus in Jerusalem, King in Memphis. They will grow up, you see, and question us. They will push back the boundaries of our knowledge, they will wonder aloud about the foundations on which we have built our power. And we can't risk that, can we?

I stopped in the middle of writing this to watch a few minutes of Oliver North's testimony before the congressional hearing. What he was saying to me was that he had to shred those documents because they might fall into enemy hands. But in his definition, you and I are the enemy. Anyone who might question the absolute rightness of what he was doing would be the enemy. Our nation, more and more, treats its citizens the way we treat our children. Those in power are the experts who cannot risk sharing with the ordinary their special knowledge—that knowledge which, if they were at liberty to share, would explain why they were above the law that they expect you and me to obey. This in the two hundredth year of the birth of the Constitution, which of all human documents regards the intelligence and judgment of ordinary people with the most respect and says that no one is above the law that governs everyone.

It's interesting how often people say to me, "Well, of course, your books aren't really for children," and think, thereby, that they have complimented me. Actually, my books are for anyone who is kind enough to read them. The great majority of those readers are, have been, and I profoundly hope will continue to be under the age of fourteen.

I got a letter once from a troubled child who poured out her anguish over her parents' divorce and her own subsequent behavior. "When I read *Gilly Hopkins,*" she said, "I realized that you were the only person in the world who could understand how I feel." Poor child, I thought, not even I understand how you feel.

And as much as you and I wish to spare our children pain and so try to pretend to ourselves that they cannot feel as deeply as we, they do hurt, they do fear, they do grieve; and even when we cannot fully understand, we who care for them must take these feelings seriously.

Gerard Manley Hopkins captures what I am trying to say in his poem "Spring and Fall: To a Young Child":

> Márgarét, are you gríeving
> Over Goldengrove unleaving?
> Leáves, líke the things of man, you
> With your fresh thoughts care for, can you?
> Áh! ás the heart grows older
> It will come to such sights colder
> By and by, nor spare a sigh
> Though worlds of wanwood leafmeal lie;
> And yet you *will* weep and know why.
> Now no matter, child, the name:
> Sórrow's spríngs áre the same.
> Nor mouth had, no nor mind, expressed
> What heart heard of, ghost guessed:
> It ís the blight man was born for,
> It is Margaret you mourn for.[2]

When the child mourns the falling of the leaves in autumn, the poet says, she is unknowingly mourning the brevity, the frailty, of her own life in the world. Now, the child cannot articulate this. She hasn't the words or the experience, but she has the feelings. She does weep without fully understanding why. "Áh! ás the heart grows older/ It will come to such sights colder. . . ." Those of us who write for the young choose the passionate heart over the cold intellect every time.

Let me read you a poem written by a twelve-year-old girl in response to *Bridge to Terabithia:*

As the stubborn stream swirls and pulls out a song,
The hillside stands in the cold dark sky.
Over the hillside stands a lonely palace.
Before it shook with joy
    But now its queen is dead
So the sour sweet wind blows the tassels of the weak
    rope,
And the tree mourns and scolds the rope,
Saying "Couldn't you have held on a little longer?"

Why do I write for children? I'm practicing. Someday, if I keep working at it, I may write a book worthy of such a reader.

Out of the Mouths of Babes

———◆———

THE POLITICAL LIFE OF CHILDREN
THE MORAL LIFE OF CHILDREN
by Robert Coles

One of Jimmy Carter's unforgivable mistakes as president was his revelation that he thought his twelve-year-old had opinions worth listening to. The public hoot that greeted this earnest statement still echoes in negative assessments of the Carter presidency. We are a nation, you see, that sentimentalizes children or dismisses them, but we do not take them seriously. Nor do we have much regard for people who do.

The author of these two books is a notable exception to this prevalent attitude. We do respect Robert Coles. Of course, Coles is a psychiatrist with the imprimatur of Harvard University, but it is not his medical or professorial credentials that have won him respect, but his work as a social observer over the last twenty-five years. And though we are not inclined to pay much attention to adults who are concerned with the young, we have been compelled by the volume and integrity of his writings to notice him, despite the fact that the heart of his work is, as he himself describes it, "listening . . . then describing what has been heard—selecting the most revealing excerpts, I hope, from the endless stories children have to tell."

Children tend not to say what we want to hear when we want to hear it, but, to the patient, perceptive adult who takes them seriously, their words are eloquent, disturbing, transforming. Most of us are not good listeners, but the moral and political life of our nation would take a giant leap forward if we were to pay close attention to this man who is.

During the past ten years, Coles, often accompanied by his wife and sons, has been observing and listening to find out how children develop morally and politically. To do so he has revisited persons he has worked with before, but, for the first time, he has taken his work beyond the bounds of his own country, returning repeatedly to South Africa, Brazil, Northern Ireland, Poland, Nicaragua, and Canada.

These two volumes on the political and moral lives of children are the result of that decade of listening, but, reading the books, it is clear that the origins of the work go back at least as far as the author's days as a psychiatric resident, because learning how to listen to children has been a long and difficult process. Often, as Coles admits, his psychoanalytic training has proved a hindrance rather than a help. In his field work that developed into *Children of Crisis,* Coles met children in situations of severe stress who were apparently coping quite well. How does a psychiatrist deal with children who have none of the symptoms he has been taught to treat?

Coles says that if his wife had had her way back in 1969 the subject of the moral life of children would have been their major preoccupation all these years. "But in my mind their 'moral life' meant their psychological ways of dealing with perplexing and even dangerous circumstances. I was not ready to chronicle the moral ups and downs of these children's lives; I wanted to show (when I paid any attention at all to the moral side of things) what kind of psychological turmoil a child's conscience can incite, or indeed, constrain, dampen."

It was more than ten years before Coles himself began actively to observe the moral life of children, though Ruby, whom he first met in New Orleans in 1961, had even then refused to fit into his psychological cubbyholes. Day after day, week after week, this six-year-old black child had walked past a line of screaming, threatening white adults to desegregate (by herself) a formerly all-white school. As a therapist, Coles kept looking for signs of the terrors he felt sure the child was experiencing. How long could she deny them? Yet Ruby endured, returning smiles for jeers, and praying for her tormenters each night before she went peacefully to sleep.

Coles's wife kept urging him to investigate this. Where did such moral strength come from? There was no proper psychological explanation. Ruby wouldn't make the first stage in psychologist Lawrence Kohlberg's scheme of moral development, but this child and other unlikely children do exist and are, as Coles makes us realize, well worth listening to. Among the children Coles came to know and marvel over are a ten-year-old Brazilian con artist whose family barely survives from one day to the next, but who has drawn the line at sexual pandering or drug dealing, and a teenage prostitute who feeds her younger brothers and sisters and gives the rest of her earnings to a Roman Catholic orphanage.

These are children for whom morality is not discussed as an academic exercise but "who were all trying to find moral answers for themselves through the daily steps they took."

To say Coles came to know a child is to say that over a period of years he visited this child repeatedly, usually in the child's own home. Unlike most social scientists, he does not give tests or fill out questionnaires, he converses with his young subjects. Sometimes the basis for the conversation is a picture the child has painted. Thirty of these paintings are included in *The Political Life of Children,* four in *The Moral Life of Children.* Because Coles's relationship with a child goes over a period of years, he can reveal how a child's attitude and/or behavior changes as he or she grows older. In the case of Ruby she continues to grow as a thoughtful and compassionate human being, but, sadly, not all the changes Coles notes in the lives of his young subjects are for the better.

That children have a political life at all is a surprise to many adults. Or if children's political concerns are acknowledged, the assumption is made that their ideas are determined by the family and community in which children live. What Coles and his wife and sons and associates began to discover as they listened to the children themselves is that while the political thoughts and actions of children are certainly influenced by the concerns of their environments, in many instances children are not simply parroting the cant of their elders but struggling with their own political concepts in the midst of influences that affect their lives.

Out of the Mouths of Babes

A reading of *The Political Life of Children* should cure any adult of a sentimental view of childhood. If hearing the words of Alice, the crippled child who is a runner for a Protestant paramilitary group in Belfast, doesn't do it, listening to the story of Lon, an orphaned Cambodian refugee, or studying the painting done by Hendrick, a young Afrikaner, surely will.

Late one night I kept my husband awake telling him the difference between the Polish children Coles interviewed and the Nicaraguan. All these children live in communist countries, but the Polish children without exception despised the Jaruzelski government as an interloping force in their beloved nation, whereas the children of Nicaragua, especially the poor, but also, if grudgingly, the sons and daughters of the rich, felt that the Sandinistas, for all their faults, had given back to the people the country the Samozas and their North American allies had stolen away. "I think the president should appoint Robert Coles as National Security Adviser," I blurted out. Now, several weeks later, in the cold light of a winter morning, I still think that is one of my better ideas.

from the *Washington Post Book World*
February 2, 1986

People I Have Known

"How do you build your characters?" It's a familiar question to those of us who write fiction, and, I suspect, one of the most uncomfortable. When someone asks me about "building characters," I'm tempted to remind them that characters are people, not models you put together with an erector set. You don't "build" people, you get to know them.

All human beings are born on a certain day in a particular place and from two parents. These are all givens. When I am beginning a book, the central character is little more than an uneasy feeling in the pit of my stomach. I spend a long time trying to understand who this person is—where he or she was born, when, and from whom.

When I was trying to start *Jacob Have I Loved,* I knew the protagonist was a girl of about fourteen, who was eaten up with jealousy for a brother or sister. That was all I had to go on in the beginning. When I discovered, quite by accident, that she lived on a tiny island in the middle of the Chesapeake Bay, I was well on my way to getting to know her.

(Incidentally, anyone who has written fiction knows that such revelatory accidents are a way of life for writers. This one involved a Christmas gift book about the Chesapeake Bay which I happened to read because I was desperate for reading material on the 29th of December. Time after time, writers stumble blindly upon the very secrets that will serve to unlock the story they are currently struggling with.)

Anyhow, as I discovered, life on a Chesapeake Bay island is different from life anywhere else in America. On Tangier and Smith (the islands upon which I modeled my imaginary island of Rass), there are families that have lived on the same narrow bits of land since well before the revolutionary war. The men of the island earn their living crabbing in the warmer months and oystering in the colder. For island people, all of life is organized about the water that surrounds them and even today cuts them off from the rest of our country. The speech of the people is unlike that of those in nearby Maryland or Virginia. Scholars think it may resemble the Elizabethan speech of colonial America. The islands were converted to Methodism in the eighteenth century and remain strongly religious communities. I could go on, but you can see how being born and spending her formative years on such an island would affect the growth of Louise Bradshaw. She could be molded by her adaptation to her environment or by her rebellion against it. Either way, the place is of vital significance to the person she is and will become.

When a character is born is another revealing point. You

can see this in life. My husband and I were born at the height of the depression. Our older boy was born soon after Kennedy was assassinated. Our younger daughter was born the year both Martin Luther King and Robert Kennedy were killed. When I am trying to get to know a character, I always ask what was happening in the world when this person was born and what effect these events might have had on his life.

Usually, I determine the date of birth of all of my central characters, not just the protagonist. This was crucial to the story in my novel *Come Sing, Jimmy Jo.* James was born in 1973, and his mother was born in 1959. "But that means . . . !" Yes, it means that Keri Su was fourteen when James was born. If I know that, I can begin to understand some of the problems that have always existed between them—why almost from birth James has looked to his grandma for mothering rather than his mother.

This leads directly to the question of parentage. When I first began writing *Jimmy Jo,* I assumed that Keri Su was James's mother, and Jerry Lee was his father. The fact that Jerry Lee was ten years older than his wife explained to some extent why he was the more responsible parent of the two. After all, he was already a grown-up when the boy was born.

But the better I got to know this family, the more I realized that there was something there that they weren't telling. Gradually, I got a picture of Keri Su, a thirteen-year-old girl from the West Virginia hills. The mountain boyfriend who has made her pregnant has run away and joined the navy to escape the wrath of the girl's hard-drinking father. Now all of the father's anger is directed toward his daughter. She runs away with nowhere to run and happens into a tiny mountain town where the Johnson Family Singers are performing at one of the local churches. The girl loves music, and she hangs around until the Johnsons, especially Grandma and Jerry Lee, realize the extent of her desperation and take her under their wings. She is a good-looking, spunky kid with a powerful singing voice, and Jerry Lee, with a mixture of admiration and pity and affection, marries her. James, the child that is born so soon afterward, is a Johnson heart and soul, made so by the love of Jerry Lee and Grandma, who share with him the special love they have for each other.

What happens, then, to the rest of the family members? There is brother Earl, who was a young adolescent when Keri Su joined the family. He has always resented Jerry Lee, who is older, wiser, nicer and, as Earl sees it, much their mother's favorite. Now his brother has married a girl Earl's own age, a girl, who under different circumstances, he might have liked to take out himself. Earl is jealous of the position Keri Su immediately achieves in the family and at the same time is attracted to her despite himself.

And what about Grandpa? He seems to take his wife for granted, but perhaps he, too, feels a wistful twinge when he sees how she dotes on Jerry Lee and on the fatherless child that their son has totally accepted as his own. Doesn't blood count for something? Grandpa wonders. Like most mountain men, he puts a lot of stock in good blood. He likes the boy and all, but it's not as if James were really his grandson.

So far nothing I've said is actually in the book. It is all in the background to the story—the life these people lived before they entered the pages of this particular book. But I have to know all of these things about the characters or run the risk that my characters will be as separate and inanimate as Barbie and Ken. If you let *living* people into a story, they will move each other. If you put in *constructed* characters, you'll have to do the moving yourself. The reader won't be fooled. He'll be able to tell which is which.

When it comes to deciding what about these people will actually be revealed on the printed page, I am guided, of course, by the story I want to tell, but also, quite particularly, by point of view. *Jacob Have I Loved* is written in the first person. The only point of view the reader is given is that of Louise, who is so jealous of her sister that she is blind to the affection that her parents, Call, the Captain, and even her sister have for her. Now I am not Louise. I can see what she cannot, and it breaks my heart to realize how much her mother loves her and to know how little Louise can understand or trust that love.

A wise reader will be aware of the narrowness of Louise's vision, but since I write principally for children and young people, I know that many of my readers will assume that Louise's badly skewed view is the correct view. I suppose I could have written the book differently to give Louise's mother and even sister Caroline a sporting chance, but then the power of Louise's jealousy would have been diminished. It would have been a different, and, I believe, weaker story.

Again, in *Come Sing, Jimmy Jo,* the story is told wholly from James's viewpoint. He's never been told about his origins, but that doesn't mean he doesn't feel the uneasiness of the other family members when the past is referred to.

Often children will ask me about the parents in my books.

"Why are they so mean?" is a question I've gotten more than a few times about Jesse Aarons's parents in the book *Bridge to Terabithia.* I use the occasion to try to help young readers understand point of view. All the parents in my stories are seen from their children's point of view, and it has been my experience that children are very seldom fair in their judgments of their parents. I hope I've sent all my questioners home to take another, more objective look not only at my book, but at their own parents, most of whom, I dare say, are like the parents in *Bridge to Terabithia,* doing the best they can under trying circumstances.

Characters are like people in another way. Some of them are very easy to get to know, others more difficult. Maime Trotter, the foster mother in *The Great Gilly Hopkins,* simply arrived one day full grown. She was so powerfully herself that the other characters in the book came to life responding to her immense loving energy. Gilly, who had spent her time before the book began cynically manipulating the people about her, had to learn how to reckon with a force greater than her own anger.

The actual appearance of one of the most important characters in *The Great Gilly Hopkins* takes up less than two pages of the text. She is Gilly's mother—the unwed flower child who gave Gilly up to foster care years before the book opens. Yet what she actually is and what Gilly dreams she is (two different things, as you might suspect) combine to help shape the troubled and troubling child, whom we first meet in the backseat of the social worker's car on the way to yet another foster home.

There is, finally, something mysterious about the life of one's characters. In my secret heart, I almost believe that one of these days I'll meet Jesse Aarons walking toward me on a downtown street. I'll recognize him at once, although he will have grown to manhood, and I'll ask him what he's been doing in the years since he built that bridge across Lark Creek.

On second thought, I probably won't ask. I'll smile and he'll nod, but I won't pry. Years ago he let me eavesdrop on his soul, but that time is past. He is entitled to his privacy now. Still, I can't help wondering.

from *The Writer*
April 1987

Do I Dare Disturb the Universe?

My grandmother was a formidable Victorian whom I feared more than I loved, and it is a matter of interest to me that I remember so many things she said when I spent so much of my childhood trying hard not to listen to her. Although I never recall her forgiving me anything, I recall with surprise and perhaps envy that she was often tolerant of strangers and near strangers whose behavior seemed unacceptable to me. Rude waitresses or testy shopgirls could always count on my grandmother's compassion. Even arrogance in the great and snobbery in the less-than-great would earn my grandmother's cover-all phrase of understanding. I was not to be offended by these seemingly obnoxious people because, according to my grandmother, their behavior was "simply a form of timidity."

Why she did not extend her understanding to me, I did not know—I, who was truly timid and would have loved to have it be the excuse for all my unlovely behavior. But in my grandmother's eyes, the rest of the world was timid; I was unregenerate.

Now whether I was and/or am unregenerate is not within my province to judge, but I can surely decide whether I am timid or not. Am I subject to fear? Easily alarmed? Timorous? Shy? Yes to all of the above. If only my grandmother could have recognized it—a near-classic case.

It was, therefore, with fear, alarm, and timorousness that I sidled up to the title of this lecture: "Do I Dare Disturb the Universe?" Certainly not. I hardly dared disturb my springer spaniel. But, then, I had a sneaking suspicion that I was looking at quite a different universe from the one Prufrock was referring to. The universe that confronted me was no sleeping spaniel. It was a universe already greatly disturbed. What could I do, puny creature that I was, that would make a perceptible stir in such a whirlwind? Better, I thought, to gather my children about me, double-lock the doors, bolt the windows, and huddle together against the elements. The trouble with this metaphor is that I knew full well that my husband and probably my children would be out there somewhere battling the storm. I have never figured out just how Chicken Little managed to get herself married to the Man of La Mancha, but there you are. While John and those I truly admire are out there where the wind blows hardest, I am in my little study typing out a story for the young. Perhaps writing a book is a form of timidity.

The irony, of course, is that try as I may, I cannot escape

the universe. And in the end, the books I write must mirror it in all its terror as well as grandeur. I am condemned to write what I see, and so the books that might have been a hiding place turn into something quite different.

> To live [says Ibsen] is to battle with troll folk
> In the vault of heart and head.
> To write is man's self-judgment,
> As Doom shall judge the dead.[1]

I have often joked that writing is cheaper than psychotherapy. But there is truth in the flippancy. Writing *is* a form of self-judgment, and so, in my books, I must battle the giants I shrink from. "There's no hiding place down here," as the old spiritual says.

From 1981 to the spring of 1983 I went about the country making speeches as I am tonight. Almost invariably during this time span someone would say, "I'm so glad you've stopped writing those historical novels." And, of course, the person had no way of knowing that lying on my desk at that minute, waiting for me to return, was the most ambitious historical novel I had ever attempted. Why? Why, when I had achieved a measure of success writing about twentieth-century America would I go back to writing about the Orient and not even the modern Orient? There are a number of answers to that question, some of which I do not know, but I think I do know some of the reasons. The first is that history is a pair of powerful eyeglasses with which to look at life. We cannot look directly at reality because our eyesight is too poor, and our hearts are too faint.

When I heard the news of Martin Luther King's death, one of the first things I did was go to the music store and buy a recording of Brahms's Requiem. The only one they had was sung in German, but that hasn't mattered over the years, for the music has helped me face death over and over again. I do not mean to say that the Requiem has become for me a kind of medicine—in case of pain take two choruses and a solo—neither would I say to anyone who is bereaved, All you have to do is put on Brahms and put up your feet. Art is never a quick cure, and it is not necessarily a comfort. But art is a means of seeing truth that cannot be observed directly, and historical fiction at its best gives us two routes to truth—the route, or eyeglasses, of history and the route, or spectacles, of art. A double whammy, if you please.

Jill Paton Walsh once said something that has been a great help to me as I think about historical fiction. She said that if you want to know what a certain period of history was like, you don't go back and read the contemporary fiction that was written in that period but the historical fiction that was written in that period. Now why should such a statement be true? Because the writer is wrestling with the giants of her own time by means of the giants in history. Or, to go back to our spectacles image, she is using history to enable her to bring the present into focus.

I was born in China and lived there for nearly eight years, but I had not felt either anxious or ready to write about my native land until after I finished *Jacob Have I Loved.* What is there in the psyche that prevents you from writing something for years, and then suddenly, without any warning, tells you that the time is ripe? I don't know. I only know that one day I had no desire to write about China, and the next day I did.

But what did I want to say about China? I was sure I didn't want to write about my childhood there. A historical novel was the obvious choice. But what period of history? Recorded history in China goes back four thousand years. I began reading a brief, general history of China, trying on the one hand to stuff four thousand years into my head and on the other, to choose from those millennia a tiny segment. I had come nearly to the end of the volume when a two-paragraph description of the Taiping Rebellion of the nineteenth century hit me between the eyes.

I suppose I must have heard of the Taiping before, but I had no memory of it. Here were a group of people in China who in 1850 were talking about the equality of men and women before God. Here were people who were saying that to harm or kill a fellow creature was against God's law. They were opposed to any sort of oppression—foot-binding, prostitution, multiple marriages, the buying and selling of human beings for any purpose. They did not kill, steal, use alcohol or opium, or bow to any graven images. Moreover, they believed that every child, regardless of sex or parentage, had a right to an education—all this at a time when in America we were still arguing whether or not God meant us to hold slaves. I was fascinated by these people. Where had they gotten their high ideals and what had become of them? And I was led into the tragic story of what happens when persons of high ideals take them into a holy crusade to save the world.

Now it is entirely possible that this short epoch in Chinese history does not speak to you about what is troubling your life, but it shouted at me. And a writer who is constantly engaged in self-judgment must write about what impinges on her own life, not try to guess what will be important to the general population a year or two or three in the future when the book will finally be published. So I embarked on a study of the Taiping, which could not, of course, begin in 1850 but had to begin at least with Confucius in about 500 B.C. It had to include the whole philosophy of history that began with him—the idea that Shang Ti, or the High God of Heaven, gave to the emperor of China a Divine Mandate, enabling him to rule over the Chinese people. In turn the emperor must rule justly, placing the needs of the people above his own needs and desires. When an emperor betrayed this heavenly trust, there would be a series of natural disasters revealing Heaven's withdrawal of the Divine Mandate. This was a signal to the peasants, the poor and the oppressed, that Heaven no longer demanded their obedience to the present emperor—they were given the right, perhaps the obligation, to overthrow the unjust rule and establish a new dynasty, which would now receive the Divine Mandate.

It was in this spirit that the Taiping arose to overthrow the despised Manchu Empire. In the early days of the movement, it was really a religious movement—a preaching to the oppressed of dignity and self-worth under God. But like almost any idealistic human movement, the impulse to spread their message was very strong. One of their early and basic declarations was, "You should not kill one innocent person or do one unrighteous act, even though it be to acquire an empire." So when they launched the campaign to conquer China, which, of course, entailed the killing of many innocent people and the committing of untold unrighteous acts, some justification of this behavior had to be made. The simplest justification was to regard their enemies as nonhuman and therefore outside the province of the care of the High God. Chinese had always regarded non-Chinese as less than human. The Taiping followed this pattern. The Manchu, or whoever supported or sided with the Manchu, were less than human—demons, in fact. One cannot be faulted for ridding the world of demons. They are by definition enemies of God, and whoever would honor God must hate his enemies. Or so the reasoning goes.

I am sure I do not have to fill in for you the consequences of such thinking. History is full of it. Every person, as well as every nation, seeks to dehumanize the adversary. We kill the nameless foe and discover later, as Oedipus did, that we are members of the same family.

Now this is a terrible truth, and in a historical novel this truth will be illustrated in terrifying and agonizing events. The writer cannot simply say, "Isn't this kind of thinking awful?" She must portray this awfulness. Along about January 1982, at the point in the story where Wang Lee is turning from a reluctant recruit into a flaming zealot, I decided I couldn't stand it any longer. I simply could not finish this book. It took me a few days longer to broach the subject to my husband. After all, by this time I had been working on this book since early 1980, and I had spent three expensive weeks in China in the fall of 1981 while he kept everything going at home. We already had one child in college and a second entering in September. We needed this book. But finally I decided there was no help for it. Facts, however painful, must be faced. I was never going to finish this book. I broke it as gently as possible, but the bitter truth could no longer be withheld. I was never, ever going to be able to finish this book. "Oh," he said. "So you've reached *that* stage."

Needless to say, I went back to my typewriter. The book would be finished. "Two pages a day," I ordered myself. "You do not get up from this chair until you have produced two pages." Now some days those margins were mighty wide, but mostly it worked. For several weeks, it was two extremely malnourished pages a day, then a bit more, until finally, toward the end of May, I had a draft.

By now you're already asking yourself the next, most logical question. Okay, you had to write this book, but what right do you have to inflict it upon the young? How do you dare disturb their universe with this disturbing tale of war and betrayal?

I have to ask myself that question all the time. As a matter of fact, within days of the publication of *Rebels of the Heavenly Kingdom* there was an article titled "Where Have All the Children Gone?" in our local paper.[2] The author, Marie Winn, lamented the fact that parents no longer seek to protect their children from the world. She pled for a restoration of the boundaries between childhood and maturity—a reassertion on the part of adults that they know what is best for children—a willingness on the part of adults to spare children experiences that are too burdensome for them.

As I thought about Ms. Winn's article, I felt some glaring omissions. She never mentioned books or, indeed, art of any sort. She never considered—at least not in the scope of this article—that art might have a role in children's lives. Bruno Bettelheim is one of the experts she accused of robbing parents of their self-confidence, but she didn't mention *The Uses of Enchantment* or its thesis that the hearing and reading of fairy tales might provide hope for the troubled and questioning child.

I think there are points in Ms. Winn's article that we adults need to consider. There is a fine line between allowing a child to know what is happening in the family and the world and simply laying one's own emotional baggage upon the child's narrow shoulders. But I think, whatever the cause, we must recognize the burden that most of our children already bear. It's significant, I think, that Ms. Winn's article, which was supposedly about children in the United States, was only about a tiny minority of our children— those who are born in middle- or upper-class white families. And even these children are frightened by forces beyond the fondest parents' control.

"Kids already know [about the nuclear threat]," a fourteen-year-old has said. "I think it's more terrifying not to talk about it. Mystery is the worst thing possible. Being left alone to deal with it—that's much more frightening."

So while my writing begins as self-judgment, it is also for children and young people who do not live in the paradise of childhood but in the same disturbed universe that I find myself in—children who do not want to be left alone to deal with the terrors they live with every day. I cannot write for myself or these children books that pretend that we live in another, more placid universe. It simply will not work for any of us.

Recently a woman challenged me to admit that my books were not really for children. "I read them," she said, "and I was stunned. The intensity of them is overwhelming. I don't believe a child could understand what they are about." But that very week a teacher had shared a book report with me, written by her class troublemaker. The report was on *The Great Gilly Hopkins.* Without a shred of either shame or modesty, I will share with you the last two sentences of the book report. "This book is a miracle," the boy said. "Mrs. Paterson knows exactly how children feel."

Now, of course, I don't know exactly how children feel. No one knows exactly how someone else feels. But I do know how I feel, and I try to stay true to those feelings.

And so, as disturbed and discouraged and as near to despair as I feel when I confront the universe as it appears to me, I do not give up hope either as a person or as a writer (as though one could divide oneself up between form and function). My primary task is not to disturb a complacent universe or to decry a chaotic one. My task is to see through the disturbance to the unity so marvelously built into the Creation—to somehow find my way through the cacophony of reality to the harmony of truth. I have said elsewhere that my task is to write the best, the truest, story I know how to write. Someone may find these two statements contradictory. I do not.

When I remember the books I loved as a child, three stand out in a particular way. The first is *The Secret Garden. The Secret Garden* is exactly the kind of book Ms. Winn would like children to read. It is a book that gives the harmony of Eden to the child reader. I adored that book when I was eight or nine. Of course, by that time I had been through bombings and had twice fled from war. I was living as an exile in a land that was foreign to me—a land that was supposed to be my homeland, but as Jean Fritz showed so well in *Homesick,* America is never quite home to the expatriate child. Mary, in *The Secret Garden,* was also an expatriate child. Perhaps this was one reason I loved the book so much, but it can't be the whole reason, because my own children loved it, too, and they hadn't just fled from war-torn China. No, I think the reason so many of us have loved that book is precisely because we are homesick for a garden we have never visited. We long for a music we have never really heard.

The second book is related to the first. It begins in a sort of Eden. This book is *The Yearling.* I'm sure I loved it when I was eleven for some of the same reasons I had loved *The Secret Garden* two years or so before. The wonderful harmony between child and beast is a reminder of Eden. But Flag dies; the harmony is destroyed. Jody must become a man and take on the responsibilities of a man. I wept over his loss, and I knew he had lost far more than a pet or even a companion. He had lost the garden, and it could not be regained. I never thought to write Miss Rawlings a letter. It never occurred to me to take her to task for killing Flag. I knew deep down that it had to happen. I was already wise by the time I was eleven. There was no way my parents could have protected me from the world as it is. I had already seen too much. What I needed was not an outer guard but an inner strength. I needed to know that one could endure the loss of Paradise. "That's what we were put on the earth to do," says Margaret Drabble, "to endeavor in the face of the impossible." This is what reading *The Yearling* helped me to do—to endeavor in the face of the impossible.

The third book I read when I was sixteen. If you read only the first two paragraphs of this book you will think you are back in Eden.

There is a lovely road that runs from Ixopo into the hills. These hills are grass-covered and rolling, and they are lovely beyond any singing of it. The road climbs seven miles into them, to Carisbrooke; and from there, if there is no mist, you look down on one of the fairest valleys of Africa. . . .

The grass is rich and matted, you cannot see the soil. It holds the rain and the mist, and they seep into the ground, feeding the streams in every kloof. It is well-tended, and not too many cattle feed upon it; not too many fires burn it, laying bare the soil. Stand unshod upon it, for the ground is holy, being even as it came from the Creator. Keep it, guard it, care for it, for it keeps men, guards men, cares for men. Destroy it and man is destroyed.[3]

The book, of course, is Alan Paton's *Cry, the Beloved Country*. South Africa is Paradise. South Africa is Hell. The difference depends not just upon the color of your skin, but it begins there. There are many children in that land whom no loving parent can protect.

Cry, the Beloved Country was a pivotal book for me. On

reading it I had to face myself in a way I never had before. I could not pretend innocence or try to throw blame elsewhere. I knew when I had finished this book that I had met the enemy and it was myself.

A novel, as Eudora Welty reminds us, "says what people are like. It doesn't know how to describe what they are *not* like, and it would waste its time if it told us what we ought to be like, since we already know that, don't we? But we may not know nearly so well what we are as when a novel of power reveals this to us. For the first time we may, as we read, see ourselves in our own situation, in some curious way reflected. By whatever way the novelist accomplishes it—there are many ways—truth is borne in on us in all its great weight and angelic lightness, and accepted as home truth."[4]

There are adults who would rather teenagers not come face to face with such agonizing home truths. But I have never been sorry that I met my shadow when I was sixteen. I'd had earlier glimpses—my grandmother certainly tried to help me see—but this was different and I knew it. This was my own truth, something that no one else could discover for me or pressure me to discover for myself. And who would have suspected that this particular book would have had such an effect on me? Certainly, no librarian, no teacher, not even my grandmother would ever have given it to me to help me see my own situation reflected. What character in the book would an American teenage girl identify with? The old black priest? The white landowner? The murdered activist? His condemned killer? And yet it was this book more than any other that enabled me to discover myself. I was shattered by my discovery, but the very devastation made a kind of healing and growth possible. A great book can do this for a reader. It can give us hope as it judges us. It gives us a place to stand even as it casts us out of Eden.

When I look at the books I have written, the first thing that I see is the outcast child searching for a place to stand. But the next thing that I see is the promise of such a place. Terabithia is the most obvious return to Eden in my books. Eden is, it seems to me, the metaphor for the universe in perfect harmony.

It is no accident of an ignorant storyteller that the temptation in the Garden of Paradise is the temptation to eat the fruit of the tree of knowledge of good and evil. When Eve tells the serpent that God has forbidden the man and woman to eat of this tree, lest they die, the serpent says: "Ye shall not surely die: For God doth know that in the day ye eat thereof, then your eyes shall be opened, and ye shall be as gods, knowing good and evil."[5] And, ironically, the tree did make the woman and man as gods. They were no longer content to play their parts in the perfect harmony of the created universe. They now stood outside of Eden. They had not known that judgment of one creature by another would rip apart the seamless garment of Creation. By choosing to be as gods, they chose apartness and dissolution and ultimately death—not the natural return of that which is of the earth to the earth—but death that is poisoned by fear. By stepping out of their place to approve of or condemn or evaluate the worth of their fellow creatures, they destroyed the harmony God intended and put all of Creation in jeopardy. We have been homesick for Eden ever since.

Perhaps this is why, against all our experience with the world, we still deep down inside crave a happy ending—a return to innocence and joy. Perhaps this is why so often we try to convince ourselves that though Eden is lost to us, surely our children are still in the Garden. But the deed has been done—not only in that mythical Paradise but throughout human history. There's no hiding place down here. There's no going back to a place of perfect harmony and innocence. As persons we chose and every day choose again to eat the fruit. We cannot do otherwise. That is the way the world is. Our condemnation is our distinction. We are as gods. We must judge between good and evil now. We have become disturbers of the universe, but with fear and trembling, knowing that we must first judge our own hearts.

When one of our sons was at Dartmouth I had a chance to hear Dr. John Kemeny speak. For those of you who know computers, I do not have to explain who Dr. Kemeny is, but for the rest of us lesser mortals, Dr. Kemeny is one of the pioneers in this whole field. With his colleagues at Dartmouth, he invented BASIC, which is the language most people in the world use when talking to a computer. He and his Dartmouth undergraduates were the first to effect time-sharing on a computer. In the question and answer period after Dr. Kemeny's talk, someone asked him if there was anything a computer would not be able eventually to do. Dr. Kemeny replied that there were two tasks for which the human brain was perfectly suited that he did not believe any computer would ever be able to accomplish. And if somehow computers were able to do these things, he hoped that no one would ever use them in these ways. The areas where the human mind must always hold sway, according to Dr. Kemeny, are the area of creativity and the area of value judgments.

I believe Dr. Kemeny is right. Both creativity and judgment belong to humanity, and although I look upon creativity as a gift and judgment as a burden, I cannot turn either over to a machine or an organization or even to another human being. When we make value or moral judgments, we *do* further disturb the already disturbed universe, we cannot escape it. But happily, in creative endeavors, we can to some degree connect with nature and with one another. In art we can recover something of the harmony of the universe. We can become reconcilers as well as judges.

Judgment will divide and disturb the already disturbed universe. It must, and we must not like Prufrock hang back cowardly when the words must be spoken, the judgment made. But something of Eden remains with us. We can still create—we can still find harmony and connection through works of the imagination. That these works in themselves will disturb and judge is true, of course. But for them to be art and not merely propaganda they must have that deep connective quality that links soul to soul.

We must remember, however, that the balance is never a neat one. The material of the novelist is neither simply judgment nor reconciliation nor even a judicious combination of the two. The material of the novelist is human experience, in which nothing is ever neatly sorted out. It's more like watching the window of the washing machine. Now the blue jeans flap into view, now the towel, now the blouse.

114

Mercy, will the jeans turn the blouse blue? And everyone knows that when you open the door, one of every pair of socks that went in will have mysteriously vanished.

Few things make me feel as helpless as the critic who demands that it all be sorted out, that I be consistent, that the message be clear and the characters exemplary—the ending happy. That's not what I'm about. There is a basic morality to what I say and an ultimate hope, but these are, as Eudora Welty says, "deep down; they are the rock on which the whole structure of more than that novel rests."[6] Morality and hope will be in my book because the only human experience I've had is my own. But, believe me, they will be mixed up with lots of other laundry, and a few socks will always come up missing.

There is a story that Karl Barth, the greatest of this century's Protestant theologians, told on himself. Barth was a great lover of Mozart and used to begin his day playing Mozart on the phonograph to clear his mind and prepare him to go to work writing his *Dogmatics*. But Barth was always troubled that Mozart in his own lifetime had despised Protestantism. One night, Barth relates, he had a dream, and in his dream he was appointed to examine Mozart in theology. Since Barth loved Mozart's music, if not his theology, he sought to make his examination as favorable as he could. But when the time came for Mozart to reply—to defend himself—Mozart remained absolutely silent.

Here we have an example of the artist as both disturber and reconciler. Please note that Mozart's art needed no justification. The music said all that could be said, and both Barth and the Mozart of his dream knew it. Mozart connected with

Barth at a level far below that of the rational argument that was Barth's accustomed language, but he also disturbed Barth. Perhaps in seeking to reconcile, the artist always disturbs as well. Eden is no longer our natural habitat. We can never simply go back. Even the Bible acknowledges this, for the final scene set after the end of the world does not take place in a garden but in a city. And cities are the products of judgment as much as they are the product of creativity.

In closing, I'd like to share a story that was given to me by the poet and author Stanley Kiesel. It seems to me to show the artist as disturber and reconciler in a rather wonderful way. "I work as a writer in the Minneapolis Public Schools," Mr. Kiesel said, "and one day I walked into an upper elementary classroom in which the teacher had told me no writing ever went on. She also warned me about Tony, the troublemaker who sat in the back row. True, he was. He made noises. Interesting noises. One of them sounded like my old hand lawn mower in Los Angeles. I asked him to come up and be my old lawn mower in Los Angeles. He was quite happy about this. Actually, he did it with éclat, mowing up and down the aisles. Other kids volunteered their machinelike noises and we had a fine time. This led easily into talking about machines and imagining ourselves and others as machines. The last twenty minutes I asked them to write down their machine fantasies. This is what Tony wrote: 'My dad broke down two years ago. First, he lost his hubcaps then he got no brakes. His gas tank started leaking so he run out of gas alot. Then serious stuff goes on like flat tires and motor conking out. Mom and I revved him up every once in a while. But no good happening. He's just a piece of junk gone somewhere we don't know. But I miss him sometimes and I'm going to be a car fixer when I'm eighteen.' "

For Tony there is no hiding place, no Eden. We cannot protect him from this disturbing universe, but he—both the disturbed and the disturbing—can be a fixer, an artist, a reconciler. So, perhaps, can we.

Through the Valley of the Shadow of Death

THE STONES CRY OUT:
A CAMBODIAN CHILDHOOD, 1975–1980
by Molyda Szymusiak

SPIRIT OF SURVIVAL
by Gail Sheehy

Remember *The Killing Fields*? Take the most terrifying scene you can bear to recall. Now remove the man struggling across that sea of rotting flesh to rejoin his family and put in his place a little girl, a child who no longer has a family, a child who has somehow perversely survived as her parents, grandparents, aunts, uncles, brothers, sisters have either perished or disappeared. Now she is fleeing across the killing fields to an unknown place, anywhere, seeking to escape a childhood of horror piled upon horror. When you have completed this exercise, you will have heard an echo of the experience out of which these two books have emerged.

Before you conclude that you could not bring yourself to read even one such book, you should know that the echo is not the whole. Yes, the horrors spoken of are unspeakable and the terrors paralyzing, but the children of these books did not only survive, they triumphed. They learned despite every grim lesson to the contrary to hold on to faith and hope and, with the horrors past, to trust again and to feel compassion.

I read *The Stones Cry Out* first, and I suggest that this is the proper order, for this story is a muted first-person account of the years of the Cambodian holocaust told by a child who lived through it. The story begins on April 15, 1975, with a motorbike ride. The countryside is aflame, but in Phnom Penh twelve-year-old Buth Keo loves to cling on behind her seventeen-year-old aunt and pretend that the tree-lined avenue is a country lane. On this particular afternoon they hear what sounds like a tire bursting, the motorbike skids to a halt, and they watch in fascinated horror as a bicycler whose head has been blown off pedals on until his bike crashes into the closed gate of the high school.

By the next day the black-clothed youth called the Khmer Rouge have entered the city, and Buth Keo's comfortable, sheltered life in a large, loving, extended family turns into a five-year nightmare. In a vain effort to survive and stay together, the family discards all evidence of their bourgeois past, including their names. For the bulk of the book Buth Keo is called Met (Comrade) Peuw. Through starvation, exhaustion, disease, and mysterious disappearances, Peuw's extended family is reduced to herself and three younger cousins. The children learn to lie and steal and work harder than adult peasants ever had to and, above all, they learn to show no emotion, for to weep at the death of a parent or to flinch at the sight of an execution or to recoil from mutilated and rotting bodies is a capital offense.

"From time to time we crossed a clearing, where we saw more corpses, heads and limbs scattered about. Each time the Yotears [Khmer Rouge overseers] burst out laughing. 'You see what happens to people who don't listen to us!'

"After seeing those horrors, I felt stronger. 'They won't get me!' I think that was when I stopped being afraid of ghosts."

If Gail Sheehy's observations in *Spirit of Survival* are true, that was also the turning point in Peuw's life, which determined her survival and led to her present life as adopted daughter of Polish émigrés living in Paris.

In an afterword to the English translation, Peuw, now Molyda Szymusiak and in her early twenties, tells where her three surviving cousins are, and adds: "This translation will permit new readers to learn of those terrible years in my homeland, as well as the story of our survival, and the power of love in the human heart."

It is a story that had to be told, for as the title hints, if those who were a part of it had not told it, the very stones would have cried it out.

Turning from this tale to Gail Sheehy's book is to begin the same story, except that the child at the center is only five years old when it begins. But suddenly on page 21 I felt as though I had stepped out from a long, dark tunnel into a bright room where the radio was blaring. At first I was jarred by the intrusion of the angst of a well-to-do American celebrity and then annoyed. What on earth was this woman whining about? Couldn't she see these valiant children struggling on and on, their nostrils never free of the stink of rotting human flesh?

Yet this annoyance is certainly one of the responses

Sheehy intends for us to feel. She even refers to the book she was writing on the day Cambodia fell, the best-selling *Passages,* as a book having to do with "Elective crises, I might call them now. Luxury crises. At the time I thought of them as universal."

By juxtaposing her own somewhat spoiled, selfish story with the terrible account of the child who halfway through the book becomes her adopted daughter, Sheehy forces all of us who are comfortable in our own good land to ask not only what we should be doing for such children, but far more significantly, what these children might be doing for us.

Because Sheehy is telling the story, she is also examining the implications. What makes it possible for one person to survive circumstances that many others cannot endure? Once having learned the skills of survival, how can the survivor learn again how to trust, how to adapt to a new life in which those skills are no longer appropriate? How can humanity be so inhumane?

This last question receives a chilling answer. We want to think that the Nazis and the Palestinian terrorists and the Khmer Rouge are somehow aberrations, not really human, or at any rate, deeply psychotic.

Sheehy observes that in pictures she has seen of the Khmer Rouge: "They look completely comfortable with themselves."

" 'Of course they were.' Mohm shrugged. . . . 'I don't think they see themselves as being cruel. They think of themselves as being very tough and absolutely right. They believe just like'—she wasn't sure if she should say this, but went ahead—'just like President Reagan speaks as the father of the country; he thinks he's doing only great things for America. They believed they were making a better society for everyone.' "

The stories of these children make us face the evil within ourselves. They make us realize that it was the American bombing and secret invasion of Cambodia that made the atmosphere ripe for the Khmer Rouge takeover. We also have to face the fact that even now our foreign policy favors the remnant of the Khmer Rouge. They are now "freedom fighters" on the borders, seeking to recapture Cambodia from Vietnam, and the very child refugees who fled their terrors are now being encouraged by our policy to leave the refugee camps of Thailand and return to fight on the side of their former tormentors. We must examine what evils our national self-righteousness has led us to commit in the past and what evils this self-righteousness urges us to continue.

We can learn, moreover, from these children that most of what we regard as crisis experiences are shamefully petty when seen in the light of their struggles. But most of all we can rejoice with them in the miraculous resiliency of the human spirit and learn from them the power of faith, hope, and love in the human heart. These are they, as the Book of Revelation says, "who have come out of the great tribulation." They may be children, but we must sit at their feet.

from the *Washington Post Book World*
June 8, 1986

On Being a Good Boss

Recently I had lunch with a young writer whom I admire extravagantly. She has the kind of vision that can see exquisite, telling details that even Eudora Welty might miss and a voice whose clarity E. B. White would admire. Someday hers will be a name all of you will recognize. I'd be consumed with envy except for one thing. I don't think I could stand to work for her boss.

But, you say, that is ridiculous. If she is a free-lance writer, she is her own boss. Exactly. I do not believe for a minute that I am a better writer than my friend, but I know I have a better boss.

Now, I haven't always had a good boss. When I started writing twenty years ago, I had an overcritical, demanding, sneering ogre at my elbow. But over the years, as I've learned more about how to write, I've also learned better how to manage my one employee. After all, if the writer is not working well, the whole company is in serious trouble. For those of you with poor labor-management relations, here are a few things I've discovered:

1. A good boss expects her worker to do the best she can and never compares her to someone else. Any boss who compares you to Leo Tolstoy would be laughed at, but how many of your bosses make snide comparisons between you and so-and-so who just got a $15,000 advance on *her* first novel?

2. A good boss sets realistic goals. Part of the job description for a manager is goal setting. Any goals set should, however, be attainable by work on the writer's part and not depend on the caprice of prize juries and even the decision of editors. It is all right, therefore, for the boss to say that the manuscript of the novel will be mailed by October 3. It is not all right for the boss to say that it will be bought by November 3, published by June 3, and receive the Pulitzer Prize by the following spring. In my company, the boss breaks up big goals into lots of little ones. On the calendar are dates when each chapter should be written (or revised) as well as the momentous day on which a project should be mailed. Also, because she is such an understanding manager, she builds in a cushion. Then if I have dental surgery or a sick child, I can still make the mailing deadline, and if nothing untoward occurs, I have the genuine delight of beating the targeted date by two weeks.

3. A good boss is understanding without being wishy-washy. She knows that there are days that you absolutely cannot get to the typewriter. But in all proper companies, sick leave and personal leave are carefully restricted. No good boss allows an employee simply to work whenever "inspired." A good boss knows that a writer who writes only when she is inspired will work three or four days a year. Books do not get written in three or four days a year. On those terrible occasions when the writer is blocked, a good boss will not berate, but will gently insist that the writer go to work as usual. The last time I suffered one of these spells, my boss told me to write two pages before getting up from the typewriter and giving up for the day. . . .

4.   A good boss reserves criticism for appropriate times. She knows that no one can work creatively and critically at the same moment. She never peers over your shoulder while you're on a first draft. In fact my boss doesn't come to work much while I'm on a first draft. I call her in for consultation, only after I've gotten through the whole story once. I have respect for her critical ability, but if I allow her to make remarks on my work when it is still tentative and fragile, she is likely to kill something before it has a chance to breathe properly. Later on, I don't mind how ruthless she becomes. She's a stickler, for example, on checking for accuracy, but if she makes me stop and do it in the middle of a thought, I may lose what I'm trying to say.

5.   A good boss provides working conditions that are as congenial as she can possibly make them. She knows that if she does not take your work seriously, no one will. She regards your privacy as important, doesn't fuss when you don't clean up after yourself every day, and tries to keep up with supplies so that you don't run out of paper or need a new ribbon in the middle of a hard morning's work. A good boss doesn't try to make you feel guilty about spending money that she knows will pay in the long run. My boss, for example, no longer insists that all first drafts be written on the back of Christmas letters, notices from school, and first drafts of earlier novels. She found that I work better on clean paper, even if it is only the first draft.

And, finally,

6. A good boss makes the worker feel good about her work. My boss, in the old days, never missed a chance to sneeringly tell me how far short I fell of her vision. Now she knows that only makes me discouraged and reluctant to try again. So when I say, "How can I write another book? I don't even know where to begin," she says to me, "Sweetie, you can begin anywhere you want to. Just try something. Anything. It's not going to be engraved in stone. You can always throw it out tomorrow."

Sometimes my boss will pick up a book I wrote long ago and read a particularly felicitous passage. "Nice, huh?" It makes me glow all over. These days, she hardly ever goes back to point out the other less cheering examples. "What's the use?" she says. "It's too late to change it." Formerly, when reviews were painful, my boss would say, "See, they've caught on to you. That's just the fatal flaw I was telling you about. Whatever made you think you could write a book?" These days she just sighs and says, "Sweetie, haven't I told you never to read reviews? Good or bad, they just take your mind off the work you're doing now.

And that is what's important. After all, *this* is going to be the best book we've ever written." See why I'm not about to trade the old girl in?

from *The Writer*
October 1984

Stories

A couple of summers ago, I was asked to lecture at Chautauqua. Now, some of you are nearly as old as I am, and you may have heard about Chautauqua from your parents and grandparents. In the stories of my childhood, Chautauqua always conjured up visions of William Jennings Bryan and the other great orators of my grandparents' era.

I was secretly delighted with the picture of myself, the naughty child that my own grandmother despaired of, lecturing in the Greco-Roman-style Hall of Philosophy of the legendary Chautauqua Institution.

The driver who met my husband and me at the Buffalo airport was not the college student–summer employee we were expecting, but a retired airline pilot whose seasonal avocation was meeting the guest lecturers and artists at the airport. The first thing he did when we got in the car was hand over huge scrapbooks he had made with news clippings, notes, and autographs of all the VIP's he'd transported over the last several summers. He had just finished telling me about the chat he and George McGovern had had the previous week regarding the possibilities of accidental nuclear war, when he turned in my direction and asked politely, "Now, what is it *you* do, exactly?"

"I write novels for children and young people," I said.

There was a silence. "Well," he said finally, "that's important—I guess." He went on to explain in the tone of many intelligent American adults that he never read novels—just scientific books and journals and some history. He didn't really have time for novels. His wife was the one who read novels. He was too polite to voice the unspoken fact that not even she would be reading children's novels.

I am always saddened by the reminder that otherwise intelligent people feel novels are peripheral to their lives. I remember with some pain a story that came out of the 1984 presidential campaign. The Washington columnist Carl Rowan wrote about a visit President Reagan had made to an aging inner-city school building in the District of Columbia.

"At the Jefferson Junior High School here Monday," the column read, "Mr. Reagan boasted that he 'attended six elementary schools and one high school. And in none of them was there a library.' [The president] truly believes that he can sell voters the idea that facilities, libraries, books do not matter, which means he thinks he also can convince parents that his reductions in federal support do not matter

—at least not where there is 'humanity' inside dilapidated, ill-supplied school buildings."[1]

I realize that anything I say in response to this story will be cloaked in my own vested interest. When schools decide that libraries are frills, the Patersons are going to have an even harder time paying the college bills. But I would like to believe it is not simply my own vested interest that is at stake here. I believe that books, that novels, are vital to that humanity that the president says he wants us to value. We are the species that tells one another stories.

When I was in college, the common idea was that the dividing line between animal and human was the ability to make tools. We have these wonderful thumbs, you see, and this allows us to make tools, so we can sharpen rocks and pitch them at rabbits. Jane Goodall has shattered that theory. Chimpanzees make tools. We have to look further. What is our distinction? Is it the ability to communicate? No, I think it's more complicated than that. As the scientist Jacob Bronowski reminds us, animals can communicate with one another, but they do not create images. Animals, you see, lack imagination, which seems to be a distinctly human gift. "The power," Bronowski says, "that man has over nature and himself, and that a dog lacks, lies in his command of imaginary experience. He alone has the symbols which fix the past and play with the future, possible and impossible."[2] In other words, we are the animal that can tell stories, and that makes all the difference.

I was lecturing at a university two years ago and had the privilege (and I use the word a bit loosely here) of having lunch with a small group of graduate students who wanted to eat with (or up) the visiting writer. Now, one young man in the group was very proud to relate how he had gone from the foolish faith of his childhood to a wonderfully sophisticated nihilism, so he felt compelled to attack me on the grounds of what he thought was my childish religiosity.

In the course of the discussion I said something about the stories of the Bible, and he screeched in delighted triumph. "So," he yelled loud enough for the entire restaurant to hear, "So! You think they're merely stories."

"If you knew what I meant by 'stories,' " I answered—and I hope in a quiet, polite, intelligent, mature manner—"if you knew what I meant by 'stories,' you would never use the word 'mere' to describe them."

Of course there are arrangements of words that *are* merely stories. But I'm concerned with stories that truly matter. How can we distinguish the meaningful from the mere? Essayist Barry Lopez says that stories should be important to us "insofar as they sustain us with illumination and heal us."[3]

Stories "sustain us with illumination." I think what Lopez means here is that stories help us to see what is true, and that visions of truth are nourishing to the human spirit.

Now, I do not believe for a moment that any one story gives us the Truth with a capital *T*, or even that the sum of all the world's stories could do so. Let me illustrate with a story.

Moses is in the wilderness and the people of Israel, whom he rescued from four hundred years of slavery are, as the King James Version has it, "murmuring"—*murmuring* being a polite, archaic term for armed mutiny. Moses is at the point of despair. He demands proof of God's presence. If he could only see God he could keep going. As Bishop Desmond Tutu said recently, "There are occasions when you say, 'Well, God, you are in charge. This is your world. But do you think you could make it *slightly* more obvious?' "[4] Moses was at one of these occasions, and, unlike the good bishop, he wanted God to make his authority more than slightly obvious. "I beseech thee," Moses prays, "shew me thy glory."[5] In secular terms what Moses was asking for was the Truth, the whole Truth, and nothing but the Truth. He was tired of muddling about in the wilderness.

At this point I need to say something about the copy editor of the Book of Exodus. In chapter 33, the fellow must have nodded off, because in verse 11 we read, "And the Lord spake to Moses face to face, as a man speaketh unto his friend." But not ten verses later, when Moses says, "Shew me thy glory," God says: "Thou canst not see my face: for there shall no man see me, and live." Then follows the good part of the story, for the Lord goes on: " 'Behold, there is a place by me, and thou shalt stand upon a rock: And it shall come to pass, while my glory passeth by, that I will put thee in a clift of the rock, and will cover thee with my hand while I pass by: And I will take away mine hand, and thou shalt see my back parts: but my face shall not be seen.' "

Isn't that a wonderful image? I'm grateful the copy editor didn't redline the contradiction. I can't picture Moses speaking face to face with God, but in that majestic covering and uncovering hand, we have protection and mercy and even humor, which may be inadvertent and the fault of the ancient translators. Still, it adds an irresistible charm to a story that we can tell and retell with awe and pleasure for another several thousand years.

But I'm not concerned here with theological insight so much as I'm trying to talk about the relation of story to truth. When it comes to Truth with a capital *T,* we will never know it in a measurable, scientific manner, and we will never be able to encompass it. But if we are very fortunate or very blessed, we might peep through the cracks of the Almighty fingers and get a glimpse of the back parts.

I think that stories give us a way of peeping through those cracks. They allow us a vision or a partial vision of what in scientific or even literary terms is unknowable.

My husband and I have four children. One day, fifteen years ago, the baby, a dimpled, loving darling who worshiped her father, turned to him and said loudly and with passion, "No!" Her father looked at me with anguish in his face. "We're not going to have to go through this with Mary, too, are we?" Yes, with Mary, too. Now Mary is eighteen, and we have, for the fourth time, gone through solo driving, waiting up at night, and an English course called Literary Analysis.

For the fourth time a child of mine has come to me and said, "Mom, when a writer writes all that stuff down, they don't know what it means, do they?"

"No," I confess each time, feeling a bit like a literary anarchist.

"We're supposed to find all these symbols and explain them. I bet the writers don't even know they're in there, right?"

"If they do," I mumble unhappily, "they're probably not very good writers."

"Then how come I have to study this stuff?"

My impulse is to yell, "So you can get an academic diploma!" But all four times I have managed to restrain myself. It's a mercy I don't have five children.

If you ask me what one of my stories is about, I will sputter and stammer and, depending on how self-controlled I am, either give you a very childish answer, "Well, it's about this girl who's jealous of her sister," Or I will cry out, "If I could tell you what it was about in one sentence, why would I have spent nearly three years and two hundred fifteen pages doing so?" In the writer's mind, the story is not divisible, explainable, reducible. "Some people," Flannery O'Connor says, "have the notion that you read the story and then climb out of it into the meaning, but for the fiction writer himself the whole story is the meaning, because it is an experience, not an abstraction."[6]

I was asked not long ago to be my own critic, to write an article for a literary journal discussing the religious symbols that occur in my work. Now, I would be surprised, not to say disturbed, if there were no religious symbols lurking about in my books. But to go poking around for them, separating them from the flesh of the story—I'd sooner have my own cadaver cut open and the various organs exposed and prodded by a first-year medical student.

I'm not speaking here about your task as reader and critic or even as teacher. Our calling is not the same. You may very well have to teach my child literary analysis with the hope that she may learn to read with care and understanding and, I pray, appreciation and joy. I notice, moreover, that even a hypersensitive storyteller like myself can, for a small monetary consideration, be persuaded to analyze other people's books for the *Washington Post* or the *New York Times*. That's the reviewer's task, and the task of the writer and the task of the reviewer are different. But even as we analyze, we must never lose sight of the whole. For it is the work in its entirety, not the bits and pieces, that "sustains us with illumination."

Let me explain: Some years ago I got a letter from a textbook editor who said that her company would like to use a section from *Bridge to Terabithia* in a proposed reader. Enclosed was the section all scrubbed up and shiny, ready for inclusion in the textbook. It was the chapter titled "Rulers of Terabithia," condensed rather considerably. As I read it, I realized that something very peculiar had happened. I can't remember every painful detail, but I know that in the original, Mrs. Myers, the country schoolteacher, says that Leslie's scuba diving is an unusual hobby—for a girl. In the expurgated version the words "for a girl" were excised, lest Mrs. Myers be deemed sexist (which of course she was). Jesse was not permitted to say, "Lord, Leslie," and the children were not to fill Pepsi bottles with water to put in their stronghold in the woods. It seemed to me—and I readily admit that I was reading with no objectivity whatsoever—it seemed to me that any detail that delineated character or made a definite statement had been removed. All the color and flavor of the story had been blanded out. There was nothing left that could have offended any right-minded adult—or, indeed, any left-minded adult.

I would like to believe that a child who loved the original story would have been horribly offended. But I'll never know, because I said to the editor in a subsequent phone call, "It seems obvious to me that this book is not suitable for textbook use." "Oh, but it is," she said. "We want to use it for the section on Expanding Your Vocabulary. It would be perfect, if only you'd let us. . . ." But I couldn't. I couldn't sacrifice my imagined world—not even in the worthy cause of vocabulary expansion.

Then there are those other letters from teachers and librarians and parents that I find far more disturbing than my bouts with textbook editors. Here is one example:

Dear Mrs. Paterson,

I was so excited to open the pages of your Newbery Award–winning book *Bridge to Terabithia.* My excitement crashed on page 2 when I found my Lord's name used irreverently. As I read on further I read other inappropriate language, "Oh, Hell, damn," etc.

Your commendable credentials indicate a Christian upbringing as a child and an alliance with the Presbyterian church as an adult, missionary to Japan, plus being the mother of four impressionable children. I would not have expected you to contribute to the gutter and unholy talk of many youth today. Why, I ask myself, would an author of this caliber feel the need to use this type language? In no way does it enhance the message, the bonds of love, warmth, etc.; it only detracts. In this day and time when television and the printed page have downgraded speech and morals we need writers of your caliber to uplift us and refresh us with the best.

I must say, I hesitate to recommend this award-winning book to my young school patrons, or to classroom teachers to read aloud, or to discriminating parents.

Why?

Yours very truly,

No matter what anyone might think, this kind of letter does not afford me a lot of laughs. It makes me search my soul. I went back to the book and looked up the passage in which most of the profanity of the book occurs to ask myself, Could it have been written otherwise?

Though no one has ever told me why *Bridge to Terabithia* is on the Banned Books List of the American Booksellers Association, I must conclude that it is because of the scene in which the inarticulate Mr. Aarons seeks to comfort his grieving son. "Hell, ain't it?" he says. I tried to comfort my son when his best friend died, and it *was* hell, though I think fire is the wrong image. Hell is not burning but utter coldness. It is the desolation, the outer darkness, the separation from the one who loves us.

Nobody has ever told me that she was uplifted or refreshed by reading *Bridge to Terabithia*. People tell me how angry they were or how much they wept. But you see, my job is not to expand vocabularies or teach proper, reverent speech, or even, in the most obvious sense, to uplift. My job is to tell a story—a story about real people who live in the world as it is. And I dare to believe that such stories, even when they are painful, have a power to illumine the reader in the way that a nice tale with exemplary characters does not. But then, I know that the only raw material I have for the stories I tell lies deep within myself, and somehow when I go inside I find there a troubled child reaching up for comfort and understanding.

A teacher in Texas explained to me what she thought her task as a teacher of reading should be. For a long time, she said, we have been trying to train stoplight readers. We ask the children to read a bit of a story, stop, and talk about it. But what we should be working for is flashlight readers— readers who take a book under the blanket with a flashlight, because they cannot bear to stop reading what may very well be the best book they have ever read. If you want illumination, friends, a flashlight will beat a stoplight every time.

The Secret Garden was one of the flashlight books of my childhood. That doesn't make me unique. I suspect many of you felt that way about it. But it occurred to me as I was working on this speech that while I was reading *The House at Pooh Corner* and *The Wind in the Willows* and *The Secret Garden* at home, at school I was plodding through Dick and Jane. Why, if I could read as well as I know now that I could at six, why was I reading "Run, Spot, run" at school? And then it dawned on me. I was not only a flashlight reader, I was a closet reader. I never told anyone at school that I already knew how to read. In those days I was too timid to open my mouth. My kindergarten teacher in Lynchburg, Virginia, certainly didn't know. She recommended my promotion to grade one on the basis of the fact that I knew how to cut with scissors, a skill I had mastered with some difficulty in kindergarten in China. I recall the first-grade teacher in Richmond raising her eyebrows over that. As well she might. If I have any gifts, they are not in the realm of manual dexterity.

And yet, suppose I had told my first-grade teacher that Dick and Jane were intellectual and emotional slugs? Would she have been pleased? A few years ago a literate first-grader I know expressed his displeasure with the curriculum, whereupon his teacher suggested to his mother that she take him to the family doctor and ask for medication to counter his hyperactivity. This particular child could sit reading for hours at a stretch. But the teacher never thought to simply send him to the library when he finished his worksheet.

I am grateful to say that I do not believe that that would happen today. There is no need for me to seek to convince you who are teachers that reading and writing are vital to education. You know that. But I do want to encourage you to feel that stories are at the center, not at the edge, of that process. They are at the center not only because stories help us shape our lives and our society but because they have the power to lure us into learning.

I am acquainted with two junior high teachers in rural Ohio who, when confronted with classrooms full of children who hated to read and read very poorly, decided to pitch out the skill-building texts and workbooks and spend the money buying novels. They bought paperback editions of books they themselves loved, a copy of each book for each student. Then they read the books aloud in class and instructed the boys and girls to follow along in their own books. "And whatever you do," they said to the students, "don't ever read ahead." Well, you don't have to be Brer Rabbit to know how effective that prohibition was. By the end of the year, they had rooms full of literate young people whose greatest delight was sharing and discussing what they had read.

I've often thought, knowing children, that prohibition might be the magic way to teach reading. Read to children as much as possible at home and at school, but absolutely outlaw their reading for themselves. Tell them they're not developmentally ready to read until they're at least ten years old, and that in the meantime you'll do all their reading for them. This would have several desirable effects. Not only would you have legions of children all over the country huddled under the covers with flashlights and the fattest books they could borrow or steal, you'd have clandestine clubs meeting in tree houses and in alleyways to trade contraband reading material ("I'll give you two *Ramonas* for one *Tuck Everlasting*") and whisper excitedly about books. Meantime, we adults are certainly not going to devote our time and energy to reading Dick and Jane or orphaned words on flash cards. We'll choose the most wonderful stories we can find, and we'll read the ones we love over and over again. Nor, my friends, will there be any stigma attached to slow starters. They're only doing as they have been told.

Okay, so it's crazy. But not totally crazy. I had lunch a couple of years ago with the composer Alice Parker. Mrs. Parker, unlike many modern composers, loves melody—the more primitive, the better. The real melodies, she says, are those that date back to the preliterate stage of cultural development. These are the melodies that resound at a deep level of consciousness. She feels that the problem with music today is that it has been so intellectualized that it can only be responded to by the part of the brain that deals with concepts. Many composers, she said, looking to make sure I was listening, are like novelists who despise story. These are the writers who spend their time performing intellectual tricks, and then when people don't like their books, they sniff angrily. "You have to work hard to appreciate me," they say.

Mrs. Parker told me that she had held a workshop for elementary school music teachers at which one teacher said she listed for herself those concepts she wanted to teach the children that year and then chose songs that would reinforce those concepts. "No, no," Mrs. Parker said. "All backwards. You choose the songs you yourself love and share those with the children. Then one day if a hand goes up and a child asks, 'Doesn't this song do thus and such?' you nod and say, 'Yes, isn't that interesting?' and go right on singing. That," she told me, "is the way to teach music."

Come Sing, Jimmy Jo is a book about a boy who is born in West Virginia, part of a musical mountain family. When I was doing research for the book, I was amazed to find countless such families—sort of hillbilly Mozarts where the children learn to play and sing as naturally as they learn to talk. They can play any instrument lying around the house because that's what everybody does. One man said he learned to play the banjo expertly because that was the one instrument his daddy told him not to touch. He was allowed to fool with any instrument in the house *except* his daddy's banjo. Music seems to seep into these kids through their pores. Nobody much can read music, but that never slows them down from making it. They learn to sing and pick the way all of us learned to talk and the way some of us learned to read—by being exposed to it all the time.

I was once introduced to a young man who at least four different people had told me was the greatest reading teacher in the state of Missouri. I find myself slightly awkward in social situations, so I did what most awkward people do, I asked a dumb question: "Everyone tells me you're the greatest reading teacher in the state of Missouri," I said. "So, what is your secret?"

The young man shifted uncomfortably from one foot to the other. "I'm not a reading specialist," he mumbled shyly. "I'm just an ordinary classroom teacher." That would have finished our conversation except no one stepped in to rescue us from each other, so we were forced to keep talking. And ten minutes later I suddenly realized that he did, indeed, have a secret. He had begun talking about books he loved. His face glowed as he spoke, and this shy, quite ordinary young man became incredibly attractive. I was thrilled when he mentioned a book I knew and could hardly wait to get my hands on the others. Nobody had to explain to me why year after year his students read more books with deeper understanding than all the other sixth-graders in the state.

Perhaps this is the way to teach children. First, we must love music or literature or mathematics or history or science so much that we cannot stand to keep that love to ourselves. Then, with energy and enthusiasm and enormous respect for the learner, we share our love.

And we don't give out love in little pieces, we give it full and running over. We don't edit or censor or predigest; we entrust it in its fullness to someone we hope will love it too. For it is the whole work that illumines, not a stop-and-go sample.

I refused last year to watch a dramatization of *Anna Karenina* because the local critic revealed the fact that Levin had been left out of the story. Well, you can't have *Anna Karenina* and leave out Levin. It just doesn't work. All you have left is another adultery gone sour, and you can get that every Friday night on "Dallas." You don't have Tolstoy's experience of truth.

At a lower level, a librarian friend of mine confessed that she tried to read *The Great Gilly Hopkins* aloud while censoring all the profanities. So, for example, Gilly says "Rats!" to which Trotter solemnly replies, "We don't take the name of the Lord in vain around here." You see the problem.

A story that is any good is all of a piece. We can turn it about and look at it from different angles, but when we start pulling out bits, we destroy its power to illumine truth for us.

When I was at the International Reading Association meeting in Philadelphia last spring, a woman introduced herself to me. "I work in a detention center for hard-core delinquents," she said. "That doesn't mean shoplifters and runaways. That means murderers and kids who have committed violent crimes. I just want you to know how much our children love your books. The other day a girl brought back a copy of *Gilly Hopkins* to the library. 'This is me,' she said."

Can you understand from this story why I can't clean up *Gilly Hopkins*? If a girl in a detention center can identify with Gilly, then perhaps she can find someone who will be Trotter for her. Isn't it more important for this child to find herself in Gilly than for the book to receive a seal of approval from polite society?

Which brings us to speak about the power of the story to heal—to, as Barry Lopez says, "repair a spirit in disarray."[7] I realize I must tackle the subject of healing very carefully. I do not have to tell you how desperately the world needs healing, how disarrayed—indeed how broken—are the spirits of nearly everyone we meet. I don't want you to think that I regard writers as literary paramedics who rush about applying tourniquets to the bleeding wounds of the world.

The word *heal* means "to make whole." This is more than patching up, it is more than simply catharsis, the purging of the emotions. We are concerned here with growing, with becoming. We don't come into this world fully human. We become human, we become whole. And contrary to what our president might imply, stories are not frills in the curriculum of life. They are vital nourishment in this process of becoming fully human, of becoming whole.

I think of the flashlight books that started me on the road to becoming human and I am awed and grateful. *The House at Pooh Corner; The Wind in the Willows; The Secret Garden; The Good Master; Peter Rabbit; Little Women; Heidi; Paddle to the Sea; The Yearling; A Tale of Two Cities; Cry, the Beloved Country;* and, of course, the Bible. I remember such books as these and I am deeply troubled by those who feel they must tailor their publishing list and their acquisition list to "what children like." How do you know what you like when you're eight or ten? You're still at the early end of the process of becoming human. We don't bow to our children's whims when it comes to physical nourishment. I don't know of any mothers who buy only sugared cereals and bubble gum for fear of imposing their own adult tastes on their impressionable young.

And, of course, the best way to cultivate their tastes is to read to them, starting at birth and keeping on and on. "Let me hear you read it" is a test. "Let me read it to you" is a gift. So as a mother and as a writer, let me urge you to read to them, read to them, read to them. For if we are careless in the matter of nourishing the imagination, the world will pay for it. The world already has.

In an essay in the *New York Times,* Kathryn Morton addresses the question of the function of fiction and concludes:

> More than just show us order in hypothetical existences, novelists give us demonstration classes in what is the ultimate work of us all, for by days and years we must create the narrative of our own lives. A pawky, artless mess we easily make of it. We pre-write Great Drama, and then, pressed for time, dash off any old thing for the published version. We labor over and constantly revise the past and the present, Monday morning quarterbacking our way through the week to find unifying principles and meaning. We hope for some pleasant repeating themes, and pray that, when finished, the whole may have something of beauty in it. It is lonely work; we are all amateurs. To glance up and see a great novelist offering a story of rare, sweet wit and grace is to feel that our heart has found its home.
>
> So you say that reading a novel is a way to kill time when the real world needs tending to. I tell you that the only world I know is the world *as* I know it, and I am still learning how to comprehend that. These books are showing me ways of being I could never have managed alone. I am not killing time, I'm trying to make a life.[8]

To illumine and make whole—I am not equal to the commission, but at least I know how important the task is, and even if the world today reverences those who make and possess the largest, sharpest rocks, I'm grateful to be in the long line of those who, reaching to be human, gathered their children about the fire and told them stories.

The Return of Bridie McShane

---◆---

HOLD ON TO LOVE
by Mollie Hunter

While children who have loved a book long to know what happened next, an adult is more likely to approach the sequel of a book that has deeply affected her with apprehension. *A Sound of Chariots,* written by Scotland's best known writer for children and young people, was published in this country in 1972. In this first book, Bridie McShane lives through the death of her father. It is, I think, the most intense book written for a young audience that I have ever read. In the nine years since I first met her, I have been haunted by Bridie—her grief, her terror of "Time's winged chariot hurrying near," and her heightened awareness of life that makes her know she must be a writer. The book ends in 1937 with Bridie leaving school at fifteen to become an apprentice in her grandfather's flower business in Edinburgh.

Hold On to Love begins a few months later when Bridie passes out during her night school English class. A classmate, Peter McKinley, has the presence of mind to call an ambulance, and it is her friendship and eventual romance with Peter that provide the framework for the story of Bridie's late adolescence. But age and responsibility have not tamed our Bridie. She is still herself. The nine-year-old who dared challenge the haughty English landowner ("my dad wasn't a bloody Red like you said. He was a revolutionary like Christ") lives on in the seventeen-year-old who will not let anyone, not even the boy she loves, claim ownership to her soul.

Passion for the written word is still part of Bridie, as well. She will write, she must write, but in *Hold On to Love,* the passion is diffused by an adolescent's confusions and romanticism. What should she write? Poetry? Drama? Prose? And then there is the real world of poverty and illness and death and betrayal and war that is always intruding upon and chastening the lovely world of the imagination. While in the hospital following her appendectomy, Bridie has an encounter with a young gypsy. Despite great pain, the woman has fought the efforts of the staff to help her. She has to be sedated before the nurses can bathe her and prepare her for surgery. But when she is brought back to the ward after her operation, she is not only perfectly tranquil, she is, Bridie decides, beautiful, like a princess who had hidden her identity with dirt and rags. When the woman steals away from the hospital during the night following her surgery, an intrigued Bridie writes a long verse drama about her. Months later, in a tabloid wrapped around the vinegared chips which she and her brother have bought for a treat, Bridie comes across the sensationalized story of a mutilated body found on the moor and realizes with horror that it must be that of the gypsy woman who had died trying to reach her camp. The woman's body, which showed signs of recent abdominal surgery, had been ravaged by crows and foxes.

"And what about the poet, Bridie McShane, in those terrible hours of the traveling woman's last journey? What about her own silly self, lying snug in bed and dreaming pretty little dreams of a Secret Princess forced to masquerade as a tinker?" Bridie determines to write the gypsy woman's story again "with all the stark tragedy there had really been to it. And this time it would be in prose, the spare, unvarnished sort of prose that alone could do proper justice to it. This time she would give the tinker woman a voice that would also be the voice of all her kind crying out that it wasn't such a poor achievement after all, to have at least died free!"

Freedom is one of the recurring cries of this book—freedom of conscience as Bridie struggles to define her own beliefs as separate both from the narrow fundamentalism and capitalism of her grandparents' faith and the agnosticism and socialist views of the father she worshiped. There is a great yearning for intellectual freedom when formal schooling must give way to earning a living. There is the freedom desired to be oneself and pursue one's dreams despite the handicaps of being female and poor in the late '30s. These individual quests for freedom are being played out against the dark threat of Hitler's rise to power and the beginning of World War II.

As often happens when a book crosses the ocean, the title gets changed. In Britain this book was called *The Dragonfly*

Years, emphasizing that this is the time in Bridie's life when ideas and feelings are darting out in hundreds of directions, and she has not yet learned to master them. By calling the book *Hold On to Love,* the American publisher is calling our attention to the fact that the book is a love story. With all the furor over teenage romance novels these days, my first impulse was to fuss about this change of name. This is not a teenage romance. But, actually, it is a love story, a very satisfying, happy-ending love story, even though the year is 1940 and the groom is a torpedoman in the British navy. Any teenage girl who picks it up, hoping for a romance, will get more than her money's worth. And if *Hold On to Love* does not totally overwhelm the reader the way *A Sound of Chariots* did, I'm not sure we should complain. That level of intensity would be almost too much to bear twice in a row. Like the many young people who have identified with her, I am grateful to know that Bridie McShane is growing up with grit and grace. In this uncertain world, no one deserves a happy ending more.

from the *Washington Post Book World*
April 8, 1984

Peace
and the Imagination

One week ago tonight I got home from a twelve-day trip to the Soviet Union. I had planned before I left what I would say tonight, because knowing myself, I knew I would be in no condition to prepare a speech for you after I returned. People have explained to me a number of times about jet lag. You only have it traveling east. Or is it traveling west? I never can remember which direction causes jet lag, so I always have it coming and going.

Then there are those books about diet. Well, it wouldn't have helped, because I who am rarely ever sick was sick the week before I left, got well long enough to cross the Atlantic, and then fell sick again in Helsinki.

By the time I got to Vilnius, Lithuania, I was, not to put too fine a point on it, not at my best. I had sent my speech ahead with the hope that the translators would have a whack at my idiomatic language before the last minute. I had been told that I would be the keynote speaker for the American delegation at the symposium, which was entitled: "A New Approach to Soviet-American Cooperation in the Field of Literature and Art for Children and Youth." But the American leaders had no idea when during the three days I would deliver the speech, and the Soviets weren't telling.

We got to the hotel where the symposium was being held at about nine in the evening, having been greeted at the airport with great fanfare by our Lithuanian hosts. At the hotel, the rest of the Soviet delegation met us with warm speeches and hugs and kisses for the Americans who had been part of the first symposium, which was held last spring at Bread Loaf in Vermont. I hadn't been able to go to Bread Loaf, but I'd met the Soviets briefly in Washington. No one, however, remembered me well enough to hug me.

I had hardly gotten to my room when the phone rang and Patty Winpenny, head of the American delegation, asked me if I had any extra copies of my speech. I had two, but they were in the luggage that had not yet been delivered from the airport. I went down to the lobby to wait for it. There were a number of Soviets milling around. We smiled shyly at each other, very conscious of the language barrier. Then a young man who had been leaning against the cashier's desk came up to me. "Katherine Paterson?" he asked, extending his hand.

He apologized for his poor English, but he was able to explain that he had read my speech and seen the publicity picture that had accompanied it. What he was eager to tell me was that he was an editor of the *Literary Gazette*. My speech began with a story that had appeared in his magazine. Where had I read it? He was obviously thrilled to have made this connection.

Now I was standing there after two days of traveling— two days in which I had been able to keep down only tea and bread. Suddenly I felt wonderful. It seemed like a miracle to me that I should be quoting a story from this man's magazine, written by one of his close friends.

I wouldn't have been quite so thrilled if I had known that up on the eighteenth floor the American leader and the Soviet leader were battling about the same speech. It was far too long and would have to be cut to twenty minutes, Mr. Likchanov was saying. Impossible, Patty Winpenny was maintaining. "If I can say what I want to say in twenty minutes," Likchanov said, "anybody can." I don't know how long the battle raged. I delivered my two copies when the luggage arrived and went on to bed. At breakfast I was told of the fight, assured that no one would stop me in the middle, and told to talk fast. I promptly went to my room and began throwing up again.

The length of my speech wasn't the only source of disagreement during the symposium. At first Likchanov said that only five Americans would be allowed to speak at all; then suddenly he changed his mind and began providing time on the agenda for Americans who hadn't even planned to speak. The result was considerable confusion.

At Jane Roche's suggestion, I'm going to share with you the speech I made in Vilnius at the symposium, sharing along the way a few more stories from our trip. And if you don't mind, I'm going to deliver it at my normal speed.

About three years ago in my local Virginia newspaper, I read a story that filled me with hope. It was the story of an old woman in the Soviet Union who had a bomb under her bed. She knew the bomb was there. She had been in the house during World War II when the bomb had come through the roof and fallen through the floor. It had lain there forty-three years, unexploded. During the immediate crisis of the war, no one had time to do anything about Bragantosova's bomb, so she patched her roof as best she could and pulled her bed over the hole in the floor.

When things began to calm down after the war, she went to the authorities and told them about her bomb. She was brushed off. "Just another of those women trying to get an apartment in one of the new buildings," they said.

From time to time over the years she would try again. Always with the same results. No one would believe her. The more time went by, the less likely her story seemed. She began to get a reputation as a local character. She was pointed out on the street as "the grandmother with her own bomb."

Finally, forty-three years after she pulled her bed over the bomb, workmen came into the area to lay telephone cable, and they were instructed, as always in Russia, to probe for buried World War II explosives. Once more Bragantosova asked them to remove her bomb. They sent a brash young lieutenant over to check. "Where's your bomb, Grandma?" he asked, smiling. "Under your bed, no doubt?"

"Yes," she agreed and led them to her five-hun-
dred-pound bomb. The local militia evacuated two
thousand people and exploded Bragantosova's bomb
and gave her an apartment in one of the new buildings.
The article in the *Literary Gazette* that reported this event
ended with a lecture. "This proves," it said, "that the
authorities should always pay attention to ordinary
citizens."

As I say, this story filled me with hope. When I first
read it, I had just written still another batch of letters
to my congressman, senators, and the president of the
United States, trying to persuade them that there was
indeed a bomb under all of our beds. None of them
seemed the slightest bit worried. The computer-written
letters I would receive in reply to my earnestly written
pleas would be like pats on the head. "There, there,
dear. Don't take on so. We in authority know what is
best."

Well, Bragantosova gave me hope. She still gives me
hope. I resolved after I read her story never to give up.
I would keep on writing letters and making phone calls
to those in authority because, after all, they *should* listen
to ordinary citizens, and I am happy to say that one of
the senators I've kept nagging over the years seems to
have begun to listen.

So I stand before you today, if not exactly the
"grandmother with the bomb under her bed," certainly
a citizen who will keep pleading with the authorities in
her own country until they begin to make the world
safer for all its children.

I am very grateful to be here with you who share my deepest concerns, and I have come to this conference not so much ready to give as eager to receive. I am painfully aware that at the present time it is the authorities in my country who are not paying attention to the rest of the world. I pray that in our time together, you will help me listen—you will share with me those concerns that you want me to take back and share with my fellow citizens and leaders.

All of us here today are concerned with books for children, and yet none of us is naive enough to believe that the problems of the world will be solved if every child learns to read. Wars today are begun by literate people. The nuclear threat that holds the world hostage is a danger invented and carried on by clever, educated minds. So we have to admit that in some ways education is a dangerous activity. Perhaps the world would be a safer place if we were still drawing pictures on the sides of caves and hunting with spears. But we can't return to ignorance, nor do we want to. Neither can we seek to control others by keeping them in ignorance. Martin Luther King, Jr., said that peace is not simply the absence of conflict, it is the presence of justice. And surely among the demands of justice is universal literacy.

One of my heroes is Frederick Douglass, a man who began his life as a slave in 1817 and became a leading abolitionist and a statesman. In his autobiography, Douglass tells this story from his childhood when he was a slave in a Maryland household:

"Very soon after I went to live with Mr. and Mrs. Auld," he says, "she very kindly commenced to teach me the A, B, C. After I had learned this, she assisted me in learning to spell words of three or four letters. Just at this point of my progress, Mr. Auld found out what was going on, and at once forbade Mrs. Auld to instruct me further, telling her among other things, that it was unlawful, as well as unsafe to teach a slave to read. . . . 'Now,' he said, 'if you teach that nigger [speaking of myself] how to read, there would be no keeping him. It would be forever unfit for him to be a slave. He would at once become unmanageable and of no value to his master. As to himself, it could do him no good, but a great deal of harm. It would make him discontented and unhappy.' . . . From that moment," Douglass says, "I understood the pathway from slavery to freedom. . . . Whilst I was saddened by the thought of losing the aid of my kind mistress, I was gladdened by the invaluable instruction which, by the merest accident, I gained from my master. Though conscious of the difficulty of learning without a teacher, I set out with high hope, and a fixed purpose, at whatever cost of trouble, to learn how to read. . . ."[1]

Now, why was Mr. Auld so upset when he found that young Frederick had learned the alphabet and a few simple words? Wouldn't it have been a help to have a house slave who could read instructions and signs? Well, of course, that was not what Mr. Auld was concerned about. What frightened him was that given half a chance, Frederick might go on and read other things—newspapers, journals, even, heaven forbid, books. Mr. Auld knew what a dangerous floodgate the skill of reading could open up. Once having tasted the freedom of the printed word, his slave would never be able to accept the bondage of his body or his spirit.

Reading, as Frederick Douglass understood, is a pathway from slavery to freedom, and freedom is an essential ingredient of justice and therefore necessary for peace.

At the symposium, we were constantly being interviewed by the Soviet press. The reporter from the news agency TASS asked me about the TV miniseries "Amerika." I hadn't watched it, I said. But I had gotten the report from people who had that it was rather boring. But wasn't I distressed, he asked, when the world so desperately needs for the superpowers to understand each other, that such a negative picture of the Soviet people be on American television? Yes, I said. I wished ABC had not chosen to do it, but when you have free speech, you must take the bad with the good.

Then I believed that people should be perfectly free to do anything they wished? he asked. And I tried to explain how freedom entails responsibility. And as I spoke, I realized what a scary thing freedom is. Even in our own country on the Bicentennial of the Constitution, the forces that feel the freedom to read should be curtailed are much louder than those that uphold that freedom, especially when it comes to children.

In order to have peace, we must have freedom, but we must also have a vision of the world that is larger than our individual or even national concerns. We must see that the world is infinitely and intricately interconnected. Nearly 2,000 years ago the apostle Paul said, "We are members one of another."[2] This is a truth that our scientists are affirming in ways Paul could not have dreamed. And it is the human imagination, as the physicist Jacob Bronowski reminds us, that allows us to discover the invisible, the hidden, connections.

Some years ago I wrote a book titled *The Great Gilly Hopkins.* It is the story of a foster child who longs for a permanent home, but like most of us, she goes about getting what she desires in all the wrong ways. She protects herself by being a loud-mouthed bully. She lies and steals and fights. I love her with all my heart.

About four years ago a group of Soviet publishers visited my New York publisher looking for books that might be translated into Russian. Someone showed them a copy of *Gilly Hopkins* and told them a little of the story. "What's a foster child?" one of the Soviets asked. The American explained. "Oh," the visitor replied, "we have no such thing in the Soviet Union."

You can imagine my surprise, therefore, when I learned that the only one of my books that had been chosen for Russian translation was *Gilly Hopkins.* What were they going to do to my book? Would they use it to show how homeless children must suffer under capitalism? I dreaded to think of it. But then, several months later, the book arrived. I can't even read my own name on the cover, but I can look at the illustrations. I can see clearly by the posture, the line, and the expressions, that at least one Soviet citizen understands exactly what *Gilly Hopkins* is all about. The warmth, the humor, the poignancy of the pictures is unmistakable. The Soviet illustrator and I have made a deep connection across all the impassable boundaries of space and language and ideology.

It was fun for me, as you can guess, to meet Soviets who had read *Gilly.* There was even a gentleman there who had written an article about *Gilly* for the chief journal of literary criticism. There were copies of the book in the Central Children's Library. And a Lithuanian publishing house is negotiating for Lithuanian rights.

In order to have peace we must be able to see connections. In order to have peace we must use our imaginations. I was at a conference in Washington State a few years ago and happened to have breakfast with one of the other speakers. The topic turned, as it often does, to politics and I trotted out my obviously biased view that those who seek to lead the United States today seem to lack imagination.

The gentleman I was talking to was a specialist in the working of the human brain. "Well," he said, "you're on the right track. It seems to me the current administration is a classic example of a body under stress." He then began to explain to me quite technically what happens to a body under stress. Those of you who know more about such things than I will probably cringe at my explanation of his explanation, but for what it's worth, this is what I heard Dr. Sylwester saying: When a body is under stress, all the energy of the organism is concentrated on saving the skin—the cholesterol level rises to repair possible cell damage, elements are released into the blood to aid clotting, the heart pumps blood faster, muscle blood flow increases, as does the rate of breathing. As a consequence, the heart is overworked while the stomach and the viscera practically shut down operations, and the brain does not have the energy to think, much less to imagine. "Look what is happening in our country," he said. "All our resources are concentrated out there on saving the skin, and, as a consequence, the inside is dying."

It seems to me that we who care about the survival of our planet must somehow cease devoting all our energies to saving our own skins. That is an exercise in despair in a nuclear age. What was appropriate for the cavemen will not work for us. Fight or flight are no longer viable options for the human race. We must devote ourselves to finding connections rather than causing or fearing divisions. We have to give the imagination a chance.

All of us here today are committed to literacy. We believe every person in the world has the basic right to learn how to read and write. But we must not be content to teach merely the decoding of words. Of course, it is good to be able to decipher street signs. It is important to determine which bus to catch to go to work. Everyone should be able to understand the directions for operating a piece of machinery. But our goal for those we teach must be much more than simple decoding. It must be true literacy—the kind of freeing experience that Frederick Douglass was talking about, when the mind is cut loose and the imagination soars.

Chimpanzees can make tools and weapons. Computers can decode and compute, but only the human mind can imagine. Our task, as persons devoted to the education of children, is to nourish the imagination. Facts are easily forgotten. Knowledge is replaced by newer information. But the ability to imagine—to make connections, to open up closed systems, to discover likenesses that have not been seen before—the ability to imagine will never become obsolete.

A woman whose son was gifted in math asked Albert Einstein how she should help her son become a mathematician. And Einstein answered, "Read him the great myths of the past—stretch his imagination."

If the basic task of education is the stretching and nourishment of the imagination, then myths, legends, and stories are, as Einstein suggested, at the center of this process.

Now, of course, I approve of this definition of education because I am a storyteller. I have been writing stories and books for children for over twenty years. But still, it is interesting to me how people do not trust me to do my job properly. Someone is always trying to tell me what kind of book I ought to write for children. Nearly always they have some moral lesson in mind that they want me to impress on my young readers. Well, I don't know about you, but when I was young, the last book I wanted to read was one that was determined to teach me a lesson.

I was a rather naughty child. I didn't really mean to be or want to be, but I seemed to be in trouble a good bit of the time. I didn't want a book that told me to be good. Everyone was always telling me to be good. My teachers, my parents, and especially my grandmother lectured me constantly on the virtues of being good. I knew quite well what good was supposed to be. My brother was good. My sister was good. My friend Betty Jean was *always* good. If being told to be good could have made a good child of me, I would have been an angel.

No, I did not want or need stories that told me to be good. What I wanted in a story was the same thing I longed for in a friend—I wanted understanding. I wanted to feel someone understood me. I wanted to understand myself. I wanted to make sense of a world that was frightening and chaotic. I didn't want a lecture, I wanted a story—a story that could make me laugh and cry and, when I had finished, would give me hope for myself and the world.

It is not enough simply to teach children to read; we have to give them something worth reading. Something that will stretch their imaginations—something that will help them make sense of their own lives and encourage them to reach out toward people whose lives are quite different from their own.

The children I write for live in a world more terrifying than the world of my childhood. Today's children have never known a time when the mushroom cloud did not form the backdrop of civilization. I once asked in a newspaper essay the rhetorical question, How do you write a book for children who do not know if there will be a world for them to grow up in? I got an answer in an angry letter to the editor that read, "Easy, lady. You don't! Leave the writing to someone who knows that children need to enjoy life as children and not have their childhood stolen from them. If you can't do that, don't write at all."

Now, I have a lot of problems with this answer, in addition to my obvious reluctance to give up my life's work. My chief problem is with the narrowness of this gentleman's concerns. When he asks that I let children enjoy life as children, he is forgetting most of the world's children—children who are hungry or cold or homeless. Children who die in dirty little wars or live in rat-infested tenements or who are beaten or cursed or neglected.

No, when a person asks that I let children enjoy childhood, he is talking about his dream children— bright, handsome, winsome, healthy, self-confident. Children who have never felt true hunger or the sting of prejudice. Children who laugh freely and know the love of a comfortable, happy family. A tiny minority of all the children who live out their lives in this world. And yet, even these, the super-blessed, cannot be left to enjoy a childhood isolated from the real world. I think we Americans were all very conscious of this when millions of our schoolchildren watched on television as their heroine schoolteacher boarded the space shuttle last year. We saw their cheers turn to horror and felt utterly helpless. We have not discovered a vaccine against fear and grief and pain. And so we find ourselves despairing of anything we could do. The world is so complex, and the problems of peace too far beyond our feeble imaginings. We cannot help ourselves. How can we hope to help our children?

In his wonderful book *Weapons and Hope,* Freeman Dyson describes the attitude of many of us to the woes of the world as the "Eeyore Syndrome."[3]

"Eeyore, the old grey Donkey, stood by the side of the stream, and looked at himself in the water.

" 'Pathetic,' he said. 'That's what it is. Pathetic.'

"He turned and walked slowly down the stream for twenty yards, splashed across it, and walked slowly back on the other side. Then he looked at himself in the water again.

" 'As I thought,' he said. 'No better from *this* side. But nobody minds. Nobody cares. Pathetic, that's what it is.' "[4]

But tragedy, Dr. Dyson maintains, is not our business. We must change our attitude toward the state of the world or perish. In his book, Dr. Dyson presents us with imaginative ways of thinking about the nuclear crisis and lays a foundation for hope, not cheap wishful thinking but hope grounded in responsible and patient endeavor. I think what he has to say relates not only to the nuclear dilemma but to all the horrendous problems that haunt our world and that both threaten and bring harm to our children. One point Dr. Dyson makes, which is particularly important for us who are concerned about children and their books, is that the best antidote for the Eeyore Syndrome is comedy.

Following Dr. Dyson's lead, let me suggest that the books our children need are comedies, and all comedies share three essential ingredients.

The first of these is sagacity. Wisdom, as Dr. Dyson suggests, would be ideal, but wisdom is in such short supply in the world that we must be content with its country cousin, sagacity. Now, sagacity has an honorable heritage in stories for children, whether we go back as far as Monkey stealing immortality from the gods or the myriad Jacks of folk and fairy tale fame. In comedy the hero may seem stupid, may be regarded as inferior by everyone he or she meets, but there is perception and judgment in comedy that will not be ultimately defeated by the plastic sophistication of the world.

In comedy there will also be humor. On the screen, large and small, there is a lot that passes for humor that is, in fact, gallows humor. Our laughter becomes a desperate last stand against despair. There is also today a kind of slapstick so cruel that we dare not examine it closely. But this is not the humor of comedy. The humor of comedy is that which allows us to keep ourselves in perspective. Stephen Leacock, the great Canadian humorist, speaks of this as the humor "that reflects through scene or character the incongruity of life itself. . . ." The kind of humor that "blends laughter and tears . . . intimately together."[5] The kind of humor to be found in the adventures of Don Quixote or Ramona Quimby.

Finally, comedy always issues in hope. Now hope is quite a different commodity from happily ever after. Happily ever after is a state of perpetual perfection where there is no room for growth or need for forgiveness. Happily ever after has no relationship to reality as we know it. But in the midst of a most imperfect world, we still hope, because hope is not a mere feeling; hope is something we do.

"You told me you would never write a book without hope," someone complained to me, "but where is the hope in *Rebels of the Heavenly Kingdom?*" They were speaking of a book I wrote that is set in China during the Taiping Rebellion in the nineteenth century.

My critic was right in the large picture. The Taiping Rebellion, which began in such high hope and with such wonderful ideals, had self-destructed, as indeed it did historically. I could not control that tragic outcome. But on the last page of the book there remain two— Wang Lee and Mei Lin—two who bear both the glory and the scars of the movement. They are living together in peace. They have not bound their daughters' feet, and they are teaching all their children to read. A miserable little remnant of hope to grow out of the scorched and ruined nation, you might think, but all true hope starts like a tiny seed that must be nurtured.

Compared to the population of the earth, we are a tiny group here today. Compared to the might of the nations we represent, we are very weak. But we are a beginning. Simply by gathering together we have begun to see a vision. For the sake of this world's children, we are making connections across all the barriers that race and nation and political ideology seek to make.

This is a time of hope for the Soviet people. Person after person said to me quietly, "These are good times for us." And the implication was that what happened next depended a lot on the United States. Gorbachev has opened a door. The Soviet people hope that we Americans will throw our bodies into that crack and force it open wider and wider, so that it can't be slammed shut ever again. Our attitude toward the Soviets is the determining factor. We don't have to agree with their economic policies which, as a matter of fact, are beginning to sound strangely like our own. We certainly don't have to approve of repression of the Jews or the war in Afghanistan. (The Soviet people themselves are daring to voice unhappiness over this war.) But we need to say both as a people and as a nation that we share a responsibility for this planet and the life upon it. I heard a lot of talk in the Soviet Union about "the big blue marble." We have to learn how to live together on what is in reality a very small planet.

I may even learn to live with Albert Likchanov. The first day went four hours without a break, and Mr. Likchanov kept up a running complaint to Patty Winpenny, who was seated next to him, about Americans who were either too well prepared and spoke too long or Americans who weren't prepared well enough to jump up and give a formal speech when he thought they ought to. The second day Likchanov gave a ten-minute break in the middle of the morning. The third day the break lasted an hour. It was, of course, during the breaks that real connections began to be made between our delegations.

When we met in Moscow on our final morning to sign an agreement for future cooperation and future symposiums, Likchanov, who had seemed so aloof in Vilnius, told a touching story. During World War II, when he was a child and his mother was working desperately to keep body and soul together, little Albert was given two gifts from America which he had never forgotten. The first was a little coat patterned like a tiger skin. It was not very warm, he said, American winters not being as harsh as winters in Russia, but he loved it. He felt very bold, very like a tiger when he wore it. And then when the family was so hungry, and his mother was working hard just to keep her children from starving, they were given powdered eggs. It was evident from the softness of his tone and the smile in his eyes that Albert Likchanov regarded those eggs as a wonderful gift.

And the gift to us who had watched this man over the past ten days was his open acknowledgment of a debt to a country he had up until then seemed to despise. Which brings me to the final story of my speech in Vilnius and this speech tonight.

We have a summer house in New York State in the foothills of the Adirondack Mountains. When we first built it, we had no immediate neighbors, so we never thought about how large our lot was or how much of the woods belonged to us. Then one summer, the lot beside ours was sold, and we suddenly became very protective of our boundaries. Where was the line that divided our property from that next to ours? Was the old apple tree ours or theirs? How much of the creek was on our land?

In New York when property is surveyed, the surveyors pound down wooden stakes and then tie orange streamers to the tops of the stakes so they can be seen at a great distance.

My husband stood at the stake near the road, and I went into the woods in search of another. The underbrush was very thick, and I was dodging the low branches of trees looking for the stake.

"I've got it!" I called to John, spying something bright orange a few feet ahead. But when I cried out, there was a flash of brilliant color across my vision. A bird, startled by my cry, flew off a dead branch and up, out of the woods. What I had taken to be proof of my ownership was a bird —a scarlet tanager. I gave up looking for my property stake.

We are members one of another. Yes, there are differences between us. Yes, there are all kinds of divisions. But peace is not won by those who fiercely guard their differences but by those who with open minds and hearts seek out connections. Therefore, our task as teachers and writers, artists and parents, is to nourish the imagination—our own and those of the children entrusted to our care. We need to be Bragantosovas warning of the bomb, but more than that we want to be scarlet tanagers, who—at the boundaries that fear and suspicion and greed have pounded into the earth—rise up, sing, and fly free.

Hope
and Happy Endings

I am very glad to be here today. I am honored to be the thirtieth recipient of this distinguished award, especially when I read the names that have preceded mine. Today is one of those occasions when I wish my Grandmother Goetchius were still alive. Grandmother would be amazed to know that I turned out something other than trifling. She used to make sweeping pronouncements that all of her children and grandchildren were *"far* above the average," but when it came down to specific children—perhaps I should say, this specific child—she despaired daily.

There was a time when I would come home from school with a book in my hand, push open the front door, and without removing my overcoat fall prone upon the living room floor, where I lay reading until suppertime. I remember one particular afternoon, my mother was quietly sweeping the rug around me. My infuriated grandmother tolerated this scene as long as she could, then came and stood over my inert body and announced to my mother in a voice tremulous with disappointment, "I'm afraid Katherine is a lover of luxury."

Usually I couldn't hear anything when I was reading, but I remember hearing that judgment and swelling up with self-righteous indignation. I was reading *A Tale of Two Cities,* for Pete's sake, Dickens—a classic. Anybody else's grandmother would be proud to have such an intellectual grandchild, thought I. But I didn't say it. We didn't argue with my grandmother. I had graduated from a church college, earned a master's degree in English Bible, become a missionary, and married a Presbyterian minister before she died, but by the time I started straightening out, she was having to be introduced to me every time we met, so I don't think she ever gave me any credit.

Actually if she were alive and in her right mind today, she'd be a hundred and twenty-one and probably fretting that this lovely medal was being presented to me in New York City by Roman Catholics. I grew up among people for whom there was something sinister, if not slightly scandalous, about consorting with Yankees and/or Catholics. The Goetchius family of Georgia traced their Calvinist roots to the Netherlands of the sixteenth century.

There's a rather bizarre legend about that first Protestant Goetchius. He was examined, condemned, and beheaded during the Inquisition. This in itself was pretty heavy stuff for me to listen to as a child, but Aunt Helen, who was telling me the story, couldn't leave it at that. "And after the ax fell," she told me, "your ancestor rose to his feet and walked three steps before he dropped dead. That," she said, "proves that a Goetchius cannot be easily defeated."

What it proved to me at twelve was that I should take my Aunt Helen's stories with a grain of salt. She was, after all, sort of the black sheep of the family—the only one of us who smoked cigarettes, played cards, and recanted the faith to live out her life as an Episcopalian.

There is another reason it is probably fortunate that my grandmother didn't live to see this day. She was a foremost proponent of the "Be sweet, my child, and let who will be clever" Southern school of raising female children. I'm sure she would have felt that for me to see my name included in the list of winners of this award would be perilous for my soul. My mother would have handled the threat with more equanimity. After I was awarded a Newbery Medal on the heels of a National Book Award, friends and family asked my mother in alarm: "What will happen to Katherine? What will all this notoriety do to her?" My mother replied, "You don't need to worry about Katherine. She has *plenty* to keep her humble."

I'm keeping in mind all those things today as you are honoring the body of my work. I love that phrase, "body of work." Actually, to be honest, I love my books. All of them. It is similar to the way I feel about my four grown children. There they are, all different, none perfect, but I look at them —bright, funny, beautiful, loving people—and I'm very grateful to have had a part in their lives. Similarly, I look at the books and they are all different, none perfect, but I reread them with affection and a sort of surprised admiration. Knowing myself as well as I do, I am always a bit amazed that I could have written them, and grateful—believe me, very grateful.

I tell myself it's all right if my books are not universally loved and admired, but of course I don't mean that, not in my heart of hearts. I want everyone to love them as I do, faults and all. Which makes this award especially welcome. It says to me that you love them all—not just one of them. But the truth of the matter is there are people who are not as kind as the Catholic Library Association—those who fail to love my books—and I have to learn to deal with that or find another line of work.

One of my coping mechanisms over the years has involved the designing of an imaginary book jacket—the jacket for the one-volume complete works of Katherine Paterson. I don't know yet what will be on the front, but the back will consist of blurbs from reviews and articles. You know those stock paperback blurbs: "Believable and moving . . ." "So and so is a breathtakingly brilliant writer." "You emerge from this marvelous novel as if from a dream, the mind on fire. . . ."

No writer I know believes those blurbs—especially the ones that have three dots preceding or following the adjectives. It is nice to have compliments in a review that make for good blurbs on your paperback, but those are not what a writer remembers. The reviews that stick tighter than a burr are the negative ones. Those are the ones that you need to learn how to deal with. So I am going to put them, or some of the choicest ones, on my dream jacket. Let me give you a sampling: "Gilly Hopkins is a robot constructed for the purpose of instructing the young." "Pompous, pretentious, and one wonders indeed why it was ever published." ". . . exceedingly irksome." ". . . a clutter of clinched metaphors . . ." "[dot dot dot] trivial [dot dot dot]." "Sara Louise's bright new beginning moves with astonishing haste to a final dead end."

That one really smarts. Particularly, I think, because I get a lot of questions about the endings of my books. Not long ago a child asked me, "Why are your endings all so sad?" I was a bit thrown. I know sad things happen in my books, but I certainly don't perceive of them as all having sad endings. I was forced to take another look at the body of my work, or at least at the endings of my novels, and I must confess that none of them has what might be conventionally called a happy ending. But does that make them sad? Or, as one troubled mother complained to me when speaking of *Gilly Hopkins*, "totally without hope"?

Surely not. I couldn't write a book "totally without hope." I wouldn't know how. "But what do you mean by hope?" Sarah Smedman, a children's literature scholar and a nun, asked me that question last fall, and I have been mulling it over ever since. Have you noticed that about questions? The really good ones can never be answered on the spot. The better the question, the longer it will take to answer. Which makes me wonder why we expect children immediately to raise their hands and spout forth instant wisdom. Perhaps it is because we are realistic about the quality of our questions.

Anyhow, the question Sarah asked me was perfectly legitimate. What did I mean by hope? I have from time to time made sweeping pronouncements about hope as it has to do with fiction, particularly children's fiction. Sarah had every right to think, therefore, that I had already carefully thought through my own definition of the word *hope.*

I was somewhat embarrassed to hear myself defining in negatives—what I didn't mean by hope, certainly as I thought of hope in my books. I didn't mean wishful thinking. I didn't mean happily ever after, or even conventional happy endings. Certainly in the scope of a juvenile novel I didn't mean hope of heaven or the Second Coming. So what did I mean?

When some readers—especially adult readers, in my experience—define hope in children's books, they do seem to mean wishful thinking. One critic asks:

> Must Paterson's capable, imaginative protagonist-narrator in *Jacob Have I Loved,* Sara Louise Bradshaw, be forced, in the name of historical accuracy, into the same kind of quietistic and blatantly antifeminist womanhood as her mother before her? Why must we witness "Wheeze" Bradshaw cheerfully trading her hopes of medical school for marriage to a widowed farmer in an Appalachian community no less isolated by the mountains than Rass Island was by the sea, while her gifted but pusillanimous twin sister Caroline, having stolen Wheeze's old friend Call Purnell for her husband, pursues wealth and fame as an opera singer in New York? Could Paterson provide no more equitable conclusion than this to her often powerful tale of sibling jealousy and rage—for the sake not only of her narrator's aspirations but those of her teenaged female readers as well?[1]

My temptation here is to start yelling at the critic. What did you want for an ending? I want to say. Would you have been satisfied if Louise had ended up a feminist radiologist in Baltimore? Would that have made her worthy in your eyes? Or, Screebies! Can't you see that Louise is more a doctor than any M.D. you or I are ever likely to meet, limited as our doctors are to specialties and technology and frightened as they are by lawsuits? This woman is out there really doing it. She doesn't need a diploma on the wall to prove to her patients that she's qualified. She proves that every day in actual practice. And what's this about her mother? What have you got against women who make the conscious choice to be homemakers? This woman had a fine husband who loved her. She raised two terrific daughters. Which reminds me. Wherever did you get the idea that Caroline was pusillanimous? Don't you know better than to take as gospel the adolescent Louise's description of her sister? The whole portrait is done in green, for heaven's sake!

You'll be relieved to know that I haven't even written a letter to the editor of that scholarly journal. I've just quietly seethed that an intelligent scholar should so malign these people that I care for so deeply.

And as for those teenage female readers for whom he is concerned, none of them has ever complained to me about my antifeminism or indeed despised the ending that so many adult critics love to hate. I think we are dealing here with a fundamental disagreement between the young reader and the adult teacher, parent, or critic. Children do not go to novels looking for role models. They may go for adventure, for escape, for laughter, or for more serious concerns—to understand themselves, to understand others, to rehearse the experiences that someday they may live out in the flesh. But they don't go for role models. When they go to a serious novel they expect to find truth, and everyone knows that role models are ideals, not realities. They want hope rooted in reality, not wishful thinking.

The child who asked about my sad endings was asking for something different. I think she was expressing a wistful yearning we all share for happily ever after, and I am the last person to denigrate happily ever after. There is a stage in a child's development when his basic psychic diet should consist of large servings of fairy tales.

We owe Bruno Bettelheim a great debt. Most of us have known in our guts that we needed fairy tales, but Bettelheim has articulated the important role they play in children's lives. Children, he reminds us, think in sweeping extremes: "I'll never learn how to tie my shoes." "It'll kill me if I eat this squash." "I'm always going to hate Susie." "Mom, you're the most beautiful woman in the world!"—There's one four-year-old's sweeping declaration I hated to let go. "No one will ever like me ever again." "I hate you! I hate you! I hate you! I hope you die and never come back here again!" The child's fears and feelings are enormous and unrealistic, and thus he needs hopes that are enormous and unrealistic.

Nothing less than happily ever after will satisfy children who see themselves helpless and hedged in by huge and powerful persons. And so the fairy tale becomes a great source of comfort for them. By the time a child is reading fairy tales, she knows the difference between fantasy and reality. But the fairy tale gives the child hope. You are a nobody now, poor little Cinderella, but just you wait. You will show them all someday. It won't be easy, but you will grow up. You have a wicked stepmother who will try to stop you, but you also have a fairy godmother who will come to your aid. You must discipline yourself, obey the limitations that her magic lays upon you, and then someday, your prince will come and you will truly be somebody.

The hope that the fairy tale provides is a limited hope. It is, according to Bettelheim, simply the hope that the child will grow up. Realistic stories can't give a child this same hope, Bettelheim says, because "his unrealistic fears require unrealistic hopes. By comparison with the child's wishes, realistic and limited promises are experienced as deep disappointment, not as consolation. But they are all that a relatively realistic story can offer."[2]

I have to admit that I think there is a great deal of truth in this view of both realistic fiction and fairy stories. And I say this as I remember that my youngest read *Cinderella* over and over again. I know perfectly well who the wicked stepmother was, and I hope like mad that the fairy godmother is the same person in this scenario. But if I say that Bettelheim is right, then don't I have to stop writing? Even if I made a switch to fairy tales, they couldn't be the old ones, the ones buried in our primitive psyches, the ones that have the power to move a child from his infantile fears and fixations toward the relative integration and self-empowerment of adulthood.

Hope and Happy Endings

It is no use to pretend that I read *The Uses of Enchantment* before I began writing realistic fiction for children, figured out the fallacy in Bettelheim's argument, and then proceeded to write my own books on the basis of a well-thought-out philosophy. In the first place, I started writing my first novel in 1968, and *The Uses of Enchantment* wasn't published until after I had written five of my now nine novels. Even after I had read it, and found myself in essential agreement with its premises, I went right ahead and wrote the same old thing for four more novels.

I do, you see, what most writers do. I write what I can. And I never think about what I'm doing until afterward. I philosophize when questions come after the book is published. Someone asks: "Why did you do such and such?" and I wonder, "Why *did* I do such and such?" and I begin to write a speech that essentially speculates on why I did something that at the time was done totally subconsciously. This is one of those speeches.

Last month our public television station broadcast the film musical *Oliver. Oliver Twist* is a good example of *peripeteia* or reversal of fortune, which is as popular a theme in fairy tales as it is in Greek drama, and a favorite plot with Dickens. Oliver starts out as a foundling in an orphanage and ends up as the heir to the kindly Mr. Brownlow. Dickens loves to make things work out happily in the end. Sometimes, as in *Nicholas Nickleby,* he makes us positively dizzy as he whirls about tying up all the loose ends and making all the good guys delirious with newfound joy.

I first saw the film *Oliver* years ago, so I'd frankly forgotten exactly how it ended. I remembered, of course, Nancy's tragic sacrifice and Bill Sykes's horrible end. I even remembered that wonderful non-Dickensian duet that sends our beloved rogues, Fagin and the Artful Dodger, skipping out of town together to work their villainy elsewhere.

But I'd forgotten the actual ending. What would the writer do with this devastated child, who has seen his beloved Nancy savagely murdered and then been taken hostage by the killer, dragged through the slums of London, only to end up high above the narrow street on a rotting scaffold that is rocking back and forth, back and forth, as the heavy body of Bill Sykes swings below in a grotesque parody of a public hanging?

Dickens himself has no trouble turning Oliver's trauma into an almost fairy-tale happy ending. Of course it takes three chapters and twenty-eight closely printed pages to do it, but as always, Dickens manages to tie every stray thread into a splendiferous macramé of justice and joy. The evil are punished, the good are bountifully rewarded, and those in the middle repent and reap such benefits as befit their middling estate. I've often wished that Dickens could have had Virginia Buckley for an editor. The ending of *Oliver Twist* is a dramatic example of what travesties can befall a good writer with a bad editor, or, as I darkly suspect, no editor at all.

But would the writer of a modern musical handle the ending any better? Would he insist on a reprise of "Who Will Buy?" with all of London singing lustily while clicking their heels in dazzling sunlight—which would come as a blinding surprise to anyone who has ever lived in the actual gray and drizzly city?

No. The writer of the film turned away from both the excesses of Dickens and the conventions of the musical comedy form. As you may remember, the carriage draws up in front of Mr. Brownlow's house. Mr. Brownlow and an exhausted Oliver get out and walk up the front steps. The kindly housekeeper comes out to greet them and, without a word spoken, much less sung, Oliver puts his arms around her and weeps.

What a lovely ending. I wish Dickens could have seen it. No singing, no dancing, no words. Any of them would have diminished Oliver's pain. We know from the way Mr. Brownlow puts his arm lightly across the boy's shoulder as they walk up the steps and the way the housekeeper's warm arms enfold him, that Oliver will be cared for. But his pain is not trivialized, much less erased. He will grow up to be a wise and compassionate gentleman, but deep in his heart, he will bear the hunger of the workhouse and the grief of Jacob's Island to his grave.

This, I maintain, is a proper ending. Perhaps I should amend that. It is a proper ending for me. It is not, strictly speaking, a happy ending. It is certainly not happily ever after. But it is a positive demonstration of what I mean when I speak of hope in stories for children.

In order to make this clearer, I want to take you back to the Bible—to the call of Moses. You remember that God first speaks to Moses from a burning bush on the mountainside. The reason Moses is wandering around that mountain in the first place is that he's a fugitive from justice. He killed a man and then had to run before the law got him. He's living in the desert, most likely under an assumed name, working as a shepherd for his father-in-law, when God speaks to him out of a burning bush and tells him to do something totally crazy: Go back to Egypt where your picture is on the post office wanted posters, go straight to Pharoah's palace and tell him you've come to organize the free labor he has slaving away on those treasure cities he's building. Pharoah's workers are going to stage a permanent walkout because I've chosen you to march this unruly mob across the trackless desert to the country your ancestors left four hundred years ago, which is now inhabited by fierce nations who live in walled cities.

Moses is understandably reluctant. He offers a number of objections to this plan. Nothing much has been heard from God for the last four hundred years. God isn't exactly in the forefront of everybody's mind these days. If Moses starts talking to the average Israelite about God, the fellow's likely to reply, "God who?" So Moses says, "If I come to the people of Israel and say to them, 'The God of your fathers has sent me to you,' and they ask me, 'What is his name?' what shall I say to them?"[3]

All of us know enough about ancient thought to know the power of the name. If the people of Israel know God's true name, they will in a sense have power over God. But at this point in the story, something wonderful happens. God does indeed give Moses a name, but it proves to be unpronounceable and a verb to boot. "Say this to the people of Israel," God says, " 'I am who I am and I will be who I will be has sent me to you.' "[4] Here is a God of the present time—of the world as it is and also the God of what will be. Nothing will ever be the same again. Being human, we will have to pronounce something to take the place of the name of this reality. We will assign nouns and pronouns, but we won't have hold of God thereby. The One whose true name is a verb is the One in whom we live and move and have our being. It is he who has hold of us. The story also assures us that the One who is and will be hears the cries of those in distress and acts to deliver them.

As a spiritual descendant of Moses, and of the prophets and apostles who followed him, I have to think of hope in this context. We are not really optimists as the common definition goes, because we, like Moses, must be absolute realists about the world in which we find ourselves. And this world looked at squarely does not allow optimism to flourish. Hope for us cannot simply be wishful thinking, nor can it be only the desire to grow up to and take control of our own lives. Hope is a yearning rooted in reality that pulls us toward the radical biblical vision of the world remade.

Those of us who worship a God whose name is an unpronounceable verb that can be translated both "I am" and "I will be," we know that what is reality for us at this moment is not the sum total of truth. We are always being pulled toward an ultimate vision of a world where truth and justice and peace do prevail in a time when the knowledge of God will cover the earth as the waters cover the sea. It is a scene that finds humanity living in harmony with nature, and all nations beating their swords into plowshares and walking together in the light of God's glory. Now there's a happy ending for you—the only purely happy ending I know of. The Book of Revelation calls it a beginning, but that's another story.

Paul tells us all creation is standing on tiptoe waiting for the ushering in of this vision. Or, we could say, the pull of that vision draws all creation toward itself. And the movement from where we are today on this dark and shadowed planet to that cosmic burst of glory—that movement is the hope by which we live.

If we think of hope in this way, there is no way that we can tack it on the end of a story like pinning the tail on the donkey. A story for children should at least have a happy ending, some say, as though happy endings are an adequate definition of hope—as though a story for children, as distinct from a story told to adults, is incomplete without a bit of cheer pasted to the end.

So what counts as an ending in a story for children by a writer who lives by hope? In the middle of writing my latest book, *Park's Quest,* I found myself once again engaged in a search for the lost parent. I was horrified. What's with you? I asked myself. Why are you always looking for a lost parent? You had two perfectly good parents of your own who loved you and did the best they could for you under often difficult circumstances. Why this constant theme of searching or yearning for the absent parent?

I think I know at last the answer to that question. I'm not sure, as I'm never sure about these things, but I think the fact that this theme keeps coming up in my books reveals a longing—not so much for my own parents—but a yearning for the One whose name is unpronounceable but whom Jesus taught us to call Father.

So the hope of my books is the hope of yearning. It is

always incomplete, as all true hope must be. It is always in tension, rooted in this fallen earth but growing, yearning, stretching toward the new creation. I am sure that it does not satisfy children in the sense that Cinderella or Jack the Giant Killer will satisfy them. I know children need and deserve the kind of satisfaction they they may get only from the old fairy tales. For children who are still hungry for happily ever after, my endings will be invariably disappointing. Children need all kinds of stories. Other people will write the stories they can write, and I will write the stories I can write.

When I write realistic novels, I will be true as best I am able to what is. But I am, as Zechariah says, a prisoner of hope. My stories will lean toward hope as a sunflower toward the sun. The roots will be firmly in the world as I know it, but the face will turn inevitably toward the peaceable kingdom, the heavenly city, the loving parent watching and waiting for the prodigal's return. Because, by the grace of God, that is truth for me and all who share this hope.

Come to think of it, and I must confess, I didn't think of it when I was writing the book, Parkington Waddell Broughton the Fifth is a kind of prisoner to hope. He sets out on a quest to find his father who was killed in Vietnam. Neither Park nor most of my readers will know that as he pursues his quest he is living out the medieval legend of Parzival the Grail knight. In the legend as Wolfram von Eschenbach tells it,[5] the Grail knight is brought by enchantment to the castle of the Grail king. The king is suffering from a wound that will not heal, and he will only be healed on the day that the Grail knight appears and asks the question.

The young Parzival, however, is the prototype of the innocent fool. He has no idea that he is the Grail knight. When he finds himself in the mysterious castle of the Grail, he's not about to ask any questions, because he has been told by those wiser than he that a man who keeps asking questions appears to be even more of a fool than he is.

So he does not ask the question. The king is not healed. And Parzival is thrown out of the castle on his ear. In his subsequent wanderings our innocent fool becomes sadder and, if not wiser, certainly less gullible, and increasingly world-weary. Try as he will he cannot find his way back to the Grail castle. He refuses to return to Camelot, convinced that he is no longer worthy to take his seat at the Round Table.

Brought back from despair by a wise hermit, Parzival comes a second time to the Grail castle, and this time he asks the suffering king the question. "Dear Uncle," Parzival asks, "what aileth thee?" And hearing these compassionate words, the king is healed.

Thus God brings both Parzival and the wounded king to wholeness. But Wolfram, like Dickens, is not content. Teller of romances that he is, he not only proceeds to restore Parzival to his kingdom and to his beloved queen, he also baptizes all in need of baptism, marries all who need marrying, and gets them "lovely children." It is truly happily ever after for Parzival and all his kin.

Park Broughton, in my story, is also an innocent fool and a bumbling knight with no notion of what his real quest is. If you read both stories, you will see that *Park's Quest* shares many elements of Wolfram's tale—the mother who tries to keep her son from the quest, the shooting of the bird, the battle with the stranger who turns out to be a brother, the king with a wound that will not heal, the failure of the knight to ask the compassionate question, and the consequences of his failure. But I did not take the happily-ever-after ending of the old romance. I tried to give it a proper ending.

And, as you tell the children, if you want to know how it comes out you'll have to read the book yourself. Actually, I thought of reading the last two pages to you, but my husband talked me out of it. And he is right. If it is indeed a proper ending, it belongs flesh, bone, and sinew to the rest of the story. If I cut it off, it will lose its life.

So to demonstrate to Sarah Smedman and to you all what I mean by hope in my books, I want to go back to a novel I wrote more than ten years ago, to a story that I think many of you already know. A book that has been called both a "story of redemption" and a story "totally without hope."

Gilly and her grandmother have gone to meet Courtney. In five minutes, or in less than two pages, her mother manages to bring Gilly's lifetime dreams crashing to the ground. Gilly flees—first to the bathroom and then to the telephone to call Trotter and tell her she's coming home because nothing has turned out the way it's supposed to. Whereupon Trotter explains to her that happy endings are a lie, and that life "ain't supposed to be nothing, 'cept maybe tough."[6]

"If life is so bad [Gilly asks], how come you're so happy?"

"Did I say bad? I said it was tough. Nothing to make you happy like doing good on a tough job, now is there?"

"Trotter, stop preaching at me. I want to come home."

"You're home, baby. Your grandma is home."

"I want to be with you and William Ernest and Mr. Randolph."

"And leave her all alone? Could you do that?"

"Dammit, Trotter. Don't try to make a stinking Christian out of me."

"I wouldn't try to make nothing out of you." There was a quiet at the other end of the line. "Me and William Ernest and Mr. Randolph kinda like you the way you are."

"Go to hell, Trotter," Gilly said softly.

A sigh. "Well, I don't know about that. I had planned on settling permanently somewheres else."

"Trotter"—She couldn't push the word hard enough to keep the squeak out—"I love you."

"I know, baby. I love you, too."

She put the phone gently on the hook and went back into the bathroom. There she blew her nose on toilet tissue and washed her face.

By the time she got back to an impatient Courtney and a stricken Nonnie, she had herself well under control.

"Sorry to make you wait," Gilly said. "I'm ready to go home now." No clouds of glory, perhaps, but Trotter would be proud.[7]

190

Hope and Happy Endings

No happily ever after, not really a happy ending, certainly not the heavenly city, but an ending rooted in this earth and leaning in the direction of the New Jerusalem. Not perfect, but I do love it. A proper ending—at least a proper ending for me, just one more in a long line of prisoners of hope.

NOTES

The Story of My Lives

1. Ashleigh Brilliant, Hallmark Cards, 1975.
2. Henry Martin, *The New Yorker,* August 5, 1985, p. 24.
3. Deuteronomy 26:5–10 (Revised Standard Version).
4. Flannery O'Connor, "The Nature and Aim of Fiction," *Mystery and Manners,* ed. Sally and Robert Fitzgerald (New York: Farrar, Straus, & Giroux, 1969), p. 68.
5. Romans 9:13.
6. Katherine Paterson, *Jacob Have I Loved* (New York: Thomas Y. Crowell, 1980), p. 215.

Ideas

1. J. R. R. Tolkien, *The Return of the King* (New York: Ballantine Books, 1965), p. 385.

2. Jill Paton Walsh, telephone conversation with author, June 11, 1988.
3. Peter Marin, "Living in Moral Pain," *Psychology Today*, November 1981, p. 71.
4. Ursula Le Guin, "The Child and the Shadow," *The Open-hearted Audience*, ed. Virginia Haviland (Washington, D.C.: Library of Congress, 1975), pp. 112–113.
5. Le Guin, "The Child and the Shadow," p. 113.
6. Marin, "Living in Moral Pain," pp. 79–80.
7. Rainer Maria Rilke, *The Notebooks of Malte Laurids Brigge*, trans. Stephen Mitchell (New York: Vintage Books, 1985), pp. 19–20.

Sounds in the Heart

1. Gerard Manley Hopkins, "God's Grandeur," *The Harper Anthology of Poetry*, ed. John Frederick Nims (New York: Harper & Row, 1981), p. 446.

The Spying Heart

1. Genesis 3:1–5.
2. Shirley Hazzard, "We Need Silence to Find Out What We Think," *New York Times Book Review*, November 14, 1982, p. 11.
3. Sumiko Yagawa, *The Crane Wife*, trans. Katherine Paterson (New York: William Morrow, 1981), pp. 23, 25.

Why?

1. Jacob Bronowski, *The Ascent of Man* (Boston: Little, Brown, 1974), pp. 425–427.
2. Hopkins, "Spring and Fall: To a Young Child," p. 448.

Notes

Do I Dare Disturb the Universe?

1. Henrik Ibsen, quoted in Robertson Davies, *One Half of Robertson Davies* (Middlesex, England: Penguin, 1978), p. 124.
2. Marie Winn, "Where Have All the Children Gone?" *The Virginian-Pilot / Ledger-Star,* June 5, 1983.
3. Alan Paton, *Cry, the Beloved Country* (New York: Scribner's, 1950), p. 3.
4. Eudora Welty, *The Eye of the Story: Selected Essays and Reviews* (New York: Vintage Books, 1979), p. 152.
5. Genesis 3:4–5.
6. Welty, *The Eye of the Story,* p. 153.

Stories

1. Carl Rowan, "The Real Reagan Record on Education Is Dismal," *Atlanta Constitution,* September 4, 1984.
2. Bronowski, "The Reach of the Imagination," *The Norton Reader,* ed. Arthur M. Eastman et al. (New York: W. W. Norton, 1980), p. 105.
3. Barry Lopez, "Story at Anaktuvak Pass," *Harper's,* December 1984, p. 52.
4. Bishop Desmond Tutu (sermon delivered at Union Theological Seminary, New York, October 25, 1985).
5. Exodus 33:18.
6. O'Connor, "The Nature and Aim of Fiction," p. 73.
7. Lopez, "Story at Anaktuvak Pass," p. 52.
8. Kathryn Morton, "The Story-Telling Animal," *New York Times Book Review,* December 23, 1984, pp. 1–2.

Peace and the Imagination

1. Frederick Douglass, *Narrative of the Life of Frederick Douglass, an American Slave, Written by Himself* (1845; reprint, New York: Signet, 1968), p. 49.
2. Ephesians 4:25.
3. Freeman Dyson, *Weapons and Hope* (New York: Harper & Row, 1984), p. 311.
4. A. A. Milne, *Winnie-the-Pooh* (1926; reprint, New York: E. P. Dutton, 1961), p. 72.
5. Stephen Leacock, quoted in *A Handbook of Literary Terms,* comp. H. L. Yelland, S. C. Jones, and K. S. W. Easton (Boston: The Writer, 1980), p. 88.

Hope and Happy Endings

1. James Holt McGavran, Jr., "Bathrobes and Bibles, Waves and Words in Katherine Paterson's *Jacob Have I Loved,*" *Children's Literature in Education* 17 (Spring 1986), p. 3.
2. Bruno Bettelheim, *The Uses of Enchantment* (New York: Alfred A. Knopf, 1976), p. 133.
3. Exodus 3:13.
4. Exodus 3:13.
5. Wolfram von Eschenbach, *Parzival,* trans. A. T. Hatto (New York: Penguin, 1980).
6. Paterson, *The Great Gilly Hopkins* (New York: Thomas Y. Crowell, 1978), p. 147.
7. Paterson, *The Great Gilly Hopkins,* p. 148.